THE ENEMY STARS

"Watch that first step," Maclaren said, grinning. "It's a long one."

"What?" Ryerson blinked, then the circuit closed and he was no longer a man: he was a signal . . .

Despite the pill he had taken, Ryerson felt as if the bottom had dropped out of the world. He grabbed for a handhold. The soft afternoon light was gone, and he was in the receiver room on a spaceship.

He hung weightless, falling into the black sun, a thousand billion billion kilometers from Earth.

POUL ANDERSON

THE ENEMY STARS

POUL ANDERSON

New and Revised Edition

A BERKLEY BOOK

published by

BERKLEY PUBLISHING CORPORATION

This new edition is dedicated to
ASTRID and TERRY
who also fly high and far

This book first appeared in *Astounding Science Fiction*
magazine under the title ''We Have Fled Our Sea'' in
August and September, 1958.

SBN 425-03943-9

BERKLEY MEDALLION BOOKS are published by
Berkley Publishing Corporation
200 Madison Avenue
New York, N. Y. 10016

BERKLEY MEDALLION BOOK® TM 757,375

Printed in the United States of America

Berkley Medallion Edition, December, 1958
New Berkley Medallion Edition, July, 1965

New and Revised Berkley Edition, JANUARY, 1979

FOREWORD

THIS IS A comparatively old work of mine, and I would have done it rather differently nowadays. Nevertheless, with due allowance for the advantages of experience and hindsight, it still seems to me to be among my better stories. I hope you will enjoy it.

The opportunity to make a few emendations was irresistible. First, technical details which are now obsolete have been corrected as much as possible. This is doubtless of concern only to those who have a special interest in physics; still, one likes to get things right. (Of course, what is "right" in science has a way of transforming itself totally every decade or two.) Second, I've tried to smooth out awkward phrasings here and there. Both these sets of changes are minor and do not affect the narrative in any way.

It was tempting to rewrite from end to end. However, time didn't permit. Nor would I likely have done so if given the chance. Better to devote that energy to something new.

Yet—well, if nothing else, contemporary feminists are not going to feel happy about the role of women in my imaginary future, and especially not about everybody's assumption that that role is natural and inevitable. I can merely reply that it doesn't seem good to me either, but the society depicted is not a very pleasant one in most respects, and people usually take for granted that the way things are is the way things must be. You will note a measure of hope for improvement toward the end of the book.

On the positive side, I think the basic theme is, today, more timely and important than ever. From a sheerly practical point of view, it is vital for humankind to become permanently established in space. The survival of machine civilization depends on that. This makes the practical consideration a moral one too, for the alternative is the death, in horrible ways, of most of us here upon Earth, followed by the survivors returning, probably forever, to what has hitherto been the norm of history—described by Alfred Duggan as "peasants ruled by brigands." The Protectorate of my story is not that bad! And in reality, the chances are excellent that a new frontier out yonder will bring forth new civilizations better than any that ever existed before.

Support an ongoing space effort. The life you save and enhance may not only be your own, but your children's and their children's, worlds without end.

—Poul Anderson

THEY named her *Southern Cross* and launched her on the road whose end they would never see. Months afterward she was moving at half the speed of light; if enough reaction mass was to remain for deceleration and maneuver, the blast must be terminated. And so the long silence came. For four and a half centuries, the ship was to fall.

They manned her by turns, and dreamed other ships, and launched them, and saw how a few of the shortest journeys ended. Then they died.

And other men came after them. Wars flamed up and burned out; the howling peoples dwelt in smashed cities and kindled their fires with books. Conquerors followed, and conquerors of those, an empire killed its mother aborning, a religion called men to strange hilltops, a new race and a new state bestrode the Earth. But still the ships fell upward through night, and always there were men to stand watch upon them. Sometimes the men wore peaked caps and comets, sometimes steel helmets, sometimes decorous gray cowls, eventually blue berets with winged stars; but always they watched the ships, and more and more often as the decades passed they brought their craft to new harbors.

After ten generations, the *Southern Cross* was not quite halfway to her own goal, though she was the farthest from Earth of any human work. She was showing a little wear, here a scratch, there a patch, and not all the graffiti of bored and lonely men rubbed out by their successors. But those fields and particles which served her for eye, brain, nerve still swept heaven; each man at the end of his watch took a box of microplates with him as he made the hundred-light-year stride to Earth's Moon. Much of this was lost, or gathered dust, in the century when Earthmen were busy surviving. But a time arrived when a patient electrically seeing machine ran through many such plates from many ships. And so it condemned certain people to death.

1

SUNDOWN BURNED ACROSS great waters. Far to the west, the clouds banked tall above New Zealand threw hot gold into the sky. In that direction, the sea was too bright to look upon. Eastward it faded through green and royal blue to night, where the first stars trod forth and trembled. There was barely enough wind to ruffle the surface, send wavelets lapping against the hull of the ketch, flow down the idle mainsail, and stir the girl's loosened pale hair.

Terangi Maclaren pointed north. "The kelp beds are that way," he drawled. "Main source of the family income, y' know. They mutate, crossbreed, and get seaweed which furnishes all kinds of useful products. It's beyond me, thank the honorable ancestors. Biochemistry is an organized mess. I'll stick to something simple, like the degenerate nucleus."

3

The girl giggled. "And if it isn't degenerate, will you make it so?" she asked.

She was a technic like himself, of course; he would never have let a common on his boat, since a few machines were, in effect, a sizable crew. Her rank was higher than his, so high that no one in her family worked productively—whereas Maclaren was one of the few in his who did not. She was of a carefully selected mutant Burmese strain, with amber skin, exquisite small features, and greenish-blond hair. Maclaren had been angling for weeks to get her alone like this. Not that General Feng, her drug-torpid null of a guardian, cared what scandal she made, flying about the planet without so much as an amazon for chaperone. But she was more a creature of the Citadel and its hectic lights than of the sunset ocean.

Maclaren chuckled. "I wasn't swearing at the nucleus," he said. "Degeneracy is a state of matter under certain extreme conditions. Not too well understood, even after three hundred years of quantum theory. But I wander, and I would rather wonder. At you, naturally."

He padded barefoot across the deck and sat down by her. He was a tall man in his early thirties, slender, with wide shoulders and big hands, dark-haired and brown-skinned like all Oceanians; but he bore an aquiline beak on the broad high-cheeked face, and some forgotten English ancestor looked out of hazel eyes. Like her, he wore merely an informal sarong and a few jewels.

"You're talking like a scholar, Terangi," she said. It was not a compliment. A growing element in the richest families found Confucius, Plato, Einstein, and the other classics a thundering bore.

"Oh, but I am one," said Maclaren. "You'd be amazed how parched and stuffy I can get. Why, as a student—"

"No, wait, you were the amateur swimwrestling

champion!'' she protested.

"True. I could also drink any two men under the table and knew every dive on Earth and the Moon. However, d' you imagine my father—bless his dreary collection of old-fashioned virtues—would have subsidized me these many years if I didn't bring some credit to the family? It's kudos, having an astrophysicist for a son. Even if I am a rather expensive astrophysicist." He grinned through the gathering dusk. "Every so often, when I'd been on a particularly outrageous binge, he would threaten to cut my allowance off. Then I'd have no choice but to come up with a new observation or a brilliant new theory, or at least a book."

She snuggled a little closer. "Is that why you are going out to space now?" she asked.

"Well, no," said Maclaren. "That's purely my own idea. My notion of fun. I told you I was getting stuffy in my dotage."

"We haven't seen you very often in the Citadel, the last few years," she agreed. "And you were so busy when you did show."

"Politics, of a sort. The ship's course couldn't be changed without an order from a reluctant Exploration Authority, which meant bribing the right people, heading off the opposition, wheedling the Protector himself—d' you know, I discovered it was fun. I might actually take up politics as a hobby, when I get back."

"How long will you be gone?" she asked.

"Can't say for certain, but probably about a month. That ought to furnish me with material for several years of study. Might dash back to the ship at odd moments for the rest of my life, of course. It'll take up permanent residence around that star."

"Couldn't you come home . . . every night?" she murmured.

"Don't tempt me," he groaned. "I can't. One

month is the standard minimum watch on an interstellar vessel, barring emergencies. You see, every
transmission uses up a Frank tube, which costs
money.''

"Well,'' she pouted, "if you think so much of an
old dead star—''

"You don't understand, your gorgeousness. This
is the first chance anyone has ever had, in more than
two centuries of space travel, to get a close look at a
truly burned-out star. There was even some argument
whether the class existed. Is the universe old enough
for any sun to have used up its nuclear *and*
gravitational energy? By the ancestors, it's con-
ceivable this one is left over from some previous cycle
of creation!''

He felt a stiffening in her body, as if she resented
his talk of what she neither understood nor cared
about. And for a moment he resented her. She didn't
really care about this boat either, or him, or anything
except her own lovely shell. . . . Why was he wasting
time in the old worn routines, when he should be
studying and preparing—oh, hell, he knew precisely
why.

And then her rigidity melted in a little shudder. He
glanced at her. She was a shadow with a palely
glowing mane, in the deep blue twilight. The last em-
bers of sun were almost gone, and one star after
another woke overhead; soon the sky would be
crowded with their keenness.

Almost, she whispered: "Where is this spaceship,
now?''

A bit startled, he pointed at the first tracings of the
Southern Cross. "That way,'' he said. "She was
originally bound for Alpha Crucis, and hasn't been
diverted very much off that course. Since she's a
good thirty parsecs out, we wouldn't notice the difference if we could see that far.''

"But we can't. Not ever. The light would take a

hundred years, and I . . . we would all be dead
— No!''

He soothed her, a most pleasant proceeding which
became still more pleasant as the night went on. And
they were on his yacht, which had borne his love
from the first day he took the tiller, in a calm sea,
with wine and small sandwiches, and presently she
asked him to play his guitar and sing. But somehow it
was not the episode he had awaited. He kept thinking
of this or that preparation: what had he overlooked,
what could he expect to find at the black sun?
Perhaps he was indeed under the subtle tooth of age,
or of maturity if you wanted a euphemism, or
perhaps the Southern Cross burned disturbingly
bright overhead.

2

WINTER LAY AMONG the Outer Hebrides. Day was a sullen glimmer between two darknesses, often smothered in snow. When it did not fling itself upon the rocks and burst in freezing spume, the North Atlantic rolled in heavy and gnawing. There was no real horizon; leaden waves met leaden sky and misty leaden light hid the seam. "Here is neither land nor water nor air, but a kind of mixture of them," wrote Pytheas.

The island was small. Once it had held a few fishermen, whose wives kept a sheep or two, but that was long ago. Now only one house remained, a stone cottage built centuries back and little changed. Down at the landing was a modern shelter for a sailboat, a family submarine, and a battered aircar; but it was of gray plastic and fitted into the landscape like another boulder.

David Ryerson put down his own hired vehicle there, signaled the door to open, and rolled through. He had not been on Skula for half a decade: it touched him, in a way, how his hands remembered the motions of steering into this place and how the dank interior was unaltered. As for his father— He bit back an inward fluttering, helped his bride from the car, and spread his cloak around them both as they stepped into the wind.

It howled in from the Pole, striking them so they reeled and Tamara's black locks broke free like torn banners. Ryerson thought he could almost hear the wind toning in the rock underfoot. Surely the blows of the sea did, crash after crash, through a bitter drift of flung scud. For a moment's primitive terror, he thought he heard his father's God, whom he had denied, roar in the deep. He fought his way to the cottage and laid numbed fingers on the anachronism of a corroded bronze knocker.

Magnus Ryerson opened the door and waved them in. "I'd not expected you yet," he said, which was as close as he would ever come to an apology. When he shut out the wind, quietness gaped.

This main room, brick-floored, whitewashed, irregular and solid, centered about a fireplace where peat burned low and blue. The chief concessions to the century were a radiglobe and a stunning close-up photograph of the Sirian binary. One did not count the pilot's manuals or the stones and skins and gods brought from beyond the sky; after all, any old sea captain would have kept his Bowditch and his souvenirs. The walls were lined with books as well as microspools. Most of the full-size volumes were antique, for little was printed in English these days.

Magnus Ryerson stood leaning on a cane of no

Terrestrial wood. He was a huge man, two meters tall in his youth and not greatly stooped now, with breadth and thickness to match. His nose jutted craggily from a leather skin, shoulder-length white hair, breast-length white beard. Under tangled brows, the eyes were small and frost-blue. He wore the archaic local dress, a knitted sweater and canvas trousers. It came as a shock to realize after several minutes that his right hand was artificial.

"Well," he rumbled at last, in fluent Interhuman, "so this is the bride. Tamara Suwito Ryerson, eh? Welcome, girl." There was no great warmth in his tone.

She bent her face to folded hands. "I greet you most humbly, honorable father." She was Australian, a typical high-class common of that province, fine-boned, bronze-hued, with blue-black hair and oblique brown eyes; but her beauty was typical nowhere. She had dressed with becoming modesty in a long white gown and a hooded cloak, no ornaments save a wedding band which bore the Ryerson monogram.

Magnus looked away from her, to his son. "Professor's daughter, did you say?" he murmured in English.

"Professor of symbolics," said David. He made his answer a defiance by casting it in the Interhuman which his wife understood. "We—Tamara and I—met at his home. I needed a background in symbolics to understand my own specialty and—"

"You explain too much," said Magnus dryly. "Sit."

He lowered himself into a chair. After a moment, David followed. The son was just turned twenty years old, a slender boy of average height with light complexion, thin sharp features, yellow hair, and his father's blue eyes. He wore the tunic of a science graduate, with insignia of tachyonics, self-consciously, not so used to it that he would change for an ordinary civilian blouse.

Tamara made her way into the kitchen and began preparing tea. Magnus looked after her. "Well-trained, anyhow," he grunted in English. "So I suppose her family is at least heathen, and not any of these latter-day atheists. That's somewhat."

David felt the island years, alone with his widower father, return to roost heavy upon him. He stifled an anger and said, also in English: "I couldn't have made a better match. Even from some swinish practical standpoint. Not without marrying into a technic family, and— Would you want me to do that? I'll gain technic rank on my own merits!"

"If you stay on Earth," said Magnus. "Who notices a colonial?"

"Who notices an Earthling, among ten billion others?" snapped David. "On a new planet—on Rama—a man can be himself. These stupid hereditary distinctions won't matter."

"We've room enough right here," said Magnus. "As a boy you never used to complain Skula was crowded. On the contrary."

"And I would settle down with some illiterate beefy-faced good Christian fishwife you picked for me and breed more servants for the Protectorate all my life!"

The words had come out before David thought. Now, in a kind of dismay, he waited for his father's reaction. This man had ordered him out into a winter gale, or supperless to bed, for fifteen years out of twenty. In theory the grown son was free of him, free of everyone save contractual overlords and whatever general had most recently seized the title of Protector. In practice it was not so easy. David knew with a chill that he would never have decided to emigrate without Tamara's unarrogant and unbendable will to stiffen his. He would probably never even have married her, without more than her father's consent, against the wish of his own— David gripped the worn arms of his chair.

Magnus sighed. He felt about after a pipe and tobacco pouch. "I would have preferred you to maintain residence on Earth," he said with a somehow shocking gentleness. "By the time the quarantine on Washington 5584 has been lifted, I'll be dead."

David locked his mouth. *You hoary old fraud,* he thought, *if you expect to hook me that way—*

"It's not as if you would be penned on one island for the rest of your days," said Magnus. "Why did I spend all I had saved to put my sons through the Academy? So they could be spacemen, as I was and my father and grandfather before me. Earth isn't a prison. The Earthman can go as far as the farthest ships have reached. It's the colonies are the hole. Once you go yonder to live, you never come back here."

"Is there so much to come back to?" said David. Then, after a minute, trying clumsily for reconciliation: "And father, I'm the last. Space ate them. Radiation killed Tom, a meteor got Ned, Eric made a falling star all by himself, Ian just never returned from wherever it was. Don't you want to preserve our blood in me, at least?"

"So you mean to save your own life?"

"Now wait! You know how dangerous a new planet can be. That's the reason for putting the initial settlers under thirty years of absolute quarantine. If you think I—"

"No," said Magnus. "No, you're no coward, Davy, when it comes to physical things. When you deal with people, though . . . I don't know what you're like. You don't yourself. Are you running away from man, as you've been trying to run from the Lord God Jehovah? Not as many folk on Rama as on Earth; no need to work both with and against them, as on a ship— Well." He leaned forward, the pipe smoldering in his plastic hand. "I want you to be a spaceman, aye, of course. I cannot dictate your choice. But if you would at least try it, once only, so you could honestly come back and tell me you're not born for stars and, and openness and a sky everywhere around you— Do you understand? I could let you go to your damned planet then. Not before. I would never know, otherwise, how much I had let you cheat yourself."

Silence fell between them. They heard the wind as it mourned under their eaves, and the remote snarling of the sea.

David said at last, slowly: "So that's why you . . . yes. Did you give my name to Technic Maclaren for that dark star expedition?"

Magnus nodded. "I heard from my friends in the Authority that Maclaren had gotten the *Cross* diverted from orbit. Some of them were mickle put out about it, too. After all, she was the first one sent directly toward a really remote goal, she is farther from Earth than any other ship has yet gotten, it was like breaking a tradition." He shrugged. "God knows when anyone will reach Alpha Crucis now. But I say Maclaren is right. Alpha may be an interesting triple star, but a truly cold sun means a deal more to science. At any rate, I did pull a few wires. Maclaren needs a tachyonics man to help him take his data. The post is yours if you wish it."

"I don't," said David. "How long would we be gone? A month, two months? A month from now I planned to be selecting my own estate on Rama."

"Also, you've only been wed a few weeks. Oh, yes. I understand. But you can be sent to Rama as soon as you get back; there'll be several waves of migration. You will have space pay plus exploratory bonus, some valuable experience, and," finished Magnus sardonically, "my blessing. Otherwise you can get out of my house this minute."

David hunched into his chair, as if facing an enemy. He heard Tamara move about, slow in the unfamiliar kitchen, surely more than a little frightened of this old barbarian. If he went to space, she would have to stay here, bound by a propriety which was one of the chains they had hoped to shed on Rama. It was a cheerless prospect for her, too.

And yet, thought David, the grim face before him had once turned skyward, on a spring night, telling him the names of the stars.

3

THE OTHER MAN, Ohara, was good, third-degree black. But finally his alertness wavered. He moved in unwarily, and Seiichi Nakamura threw him with a foot sweep that drew approving hisses from the audience. Seeing his chance, Nakamura pounced, got control of Ohara from the waist down by sitting on him, and applied a strangle. Ohara tried to break it, but starving lungs betrayed him. He slapped the mat when he was just short of unconsciousness. Nakamura released him and squatted waiting. Presently Ohara rose. So did the winner. They retied their belts and bowed to each other. The abbot, who was refereeing, murmured a few words which ended the match. The contestants sat down, closed their eyes, and for a while the room held nothing but meditation.

Nakamura had progressed beyond enjoying victory for its own sake. He could still exult in the esthetics of a perfect maneuver; what a delightful toy the human body is, when you know how to throw eighty struggling kilos artistically through the air! But even that, he knew, was a spiritual weakness. Judo is more than a sport, it should be a means to an end: ideally, a physical form of meditation upon the principles of Zen.

He wondered if he would ever attain that height. Rebelliously, he wondered if anyone ever had, in actual practice, for more than a few moments anyhow. . . . It was an unworthy thought. A wearer of the black belt in the fifth degree should at least have ceased inwardly barking at his betters. And now enough of the personal. It was only his mind reflecting the tension of the contest, and tension was always the enemy. His mathematical training led him to visualize fields of force, and the human soul as a differential quantity dX (where X was a function of no one knew how many variables) which applied barely enough, vanishingly small increments of action so that the great fields slid over each other and— Was this a desirable analog? He must discuss it with the abbot some time; it seemed too precise to reflect reality. For now he had better meditate upon one of the traditional paradoxes: consider the noise made by two hands clapping, and then the noise made by *one* hand clapping.

The abbot spoke another word. The several contestants on the mat bowed to him, rose, and went to the showers. The audience, yellow-robed monks and a motley group of townspeople, left their cushions and mingled cheerfully.

When Nakamura came out, his gi rolled under one arm, his short thickset body clad in plain gray coveralls, he saw the abbot talking to Diomed Umfando, chief of the local Protectorate garrison. He waited until they noticed him. Then he bowed and sucked in his breath respectfully.

"Ah," said the abbot. "A most admirable performance tonight."

"It was nothing, honorable sir," said Nakamura.

"What did you . . . yes. Indeed. You are leaving tomorrow, are you not?"

"Yes, master. On the *Southern Cross,* the expedition to the dark star. It is uncertain how long I shall be away." He laughed self-deprecatingly, as politeness required. "It is always possible that one does not return. May I humbly ask the honorable abbot that—"

"Of course," said the old man. "Your wife and children will always be under our protection, and your sons will be educated here if no better place can be found for them." He smiled. "But who can doubt that the best pilot on Sarai will return as a conqueror?"

They exchanged ritual compliments. Nakamura went about saying goodbye to various other friends. As he came to the door, he saw the tall blue-clad form of Captain Umfando. He bowed.

"I am walking back into town now," said the officer, almost apologetically. "May I request the pleasure of your company?"

"If this unworthy person can offer a moment's distraction to the noble captain."

They left together. The dojo was part of the Buddhist monastery, which stood two or three kilometers out of the town called Susa. A road went through grainfields, an empty road now, for the spectators were still drinking tea under the abbot's red roof. Nakamura and Umfando walked in silence for a while; the captain's bodyguard shouldered their rifles and followed unobtrusively.

Forty Eridani had long ago set. Its third planet, Il-Khan the giant, was near full phase, a vast golden shield blazoned with a hundred hues. Two other satellites, not much smaller than this Earth-sized Sarai on which humans dwelt, were visible. Only a few stars could shine through all that light, low in the purple sky; the fields lay drowned in amber radiance, Susa's lanterns looked feeble in the distance. Meteor trails crisscrossed heaven, as if someone wrote swift ideographs up there. On the left horizon, a sudden mountain range climbed until its peaks burned with snow. A moonbird was trilling, the fiddler insects answered, a small wind rustled in the grain. Otherwise only the scrunch of feet on gravel had voice.

"This is a lovely world," murmured Nakamura.

Captain Umfando shrugged. Wryness touched his ebony features. "I could wish it were more sociable."

"Believe me, sir, despite political differences, there is no ill-will toward you or your men personally—"

"Oh, come now," said the officer. "I am not that naïve. Sarai may begin by disliking us purely as soldiers and tax collectors for an Earth which will not let the ordinary colonist even visit it. But such feelings soon envelop the soldier himself. I've been jeered at, and mudballed by children, even out of uniform."

"It is most deplorable," said Nakamura in distress. "May I offer my apologies on behalf of my town?"

Umfando shrugged. "I'm not certain that an apology is in order. I didn't have to make a career of the Protector's army. And Earth does exploit the colonies. You hear euphemisms and excuses, but exploitation is what it amounts to."

He thought for a moment, and asked with a near despair: "But what else can Earth do?"

Nakamura said nothing. They walked on in silence for a while.

Umfando said at last, "I wish to put a rude question." When the flat face beside him showed no reluctance, he plowed ahead. "Let us not waste time on modesty. You know you're one of the finest pilots in the Guild; any Eridanian System pilot is—he has to be!—but you are the one they ask for when things get difficult. You've been on a dozen exploratory missions in new systems. It's not made you rich, but it has made you one of the most influential men on Sarai. Why do *you* treat me like a human being?"

Nakamura considered it gravely. "Well," he decided, "I cannot consider politics important enough to quarrel about."

"I see." A little embarrassed, Umfando changed the subject: "I can get you on a military transport to Batu tomorrow, if you wish. Drop you off at the 'caster station."

"Thank you, but I have already engaged passage on the regular intersatellite ferry."

"Uh . . . did you ask for the *Cross* berth?"

"No. I had served a few watches on her, of course, like everyone else. A good ship. A little outmoded now, perhaps, but well and honestly made. The Guild offered me the position, and since I had no other commitments, I accepted."

Guild offers were actually assignments for the lower ranks of spacemen, Umfando knew. A man of Nakamura's standing could have refused. But maybe the way you attained such prestige was by seldom refusing.

"Do you expect any trouble?" he asked.

"One is never certain. The great human mistake is to anticipate. The totally relaxed and unexpectant man is the one prepared for whatever may happen: he does not have to get out of an inappropriate posture before he can react."

"Ha! Maybe judo ought to be required for all pilots."

"No. I do not think the coerced mind ever really learns an art."

Nakamura saw his house ahead. It stood on the edge of town, half screened by Terrestrial bamboo. He had spent much time on the garden which surrounded it; many visitors were kind enough to call his garden beautiful. He sighed. A gracious house, a good and faithful wife, four promising children, health and achievement . . . What more could a man reasonably ask? He told himself that his remembrances of Kyoto were hazed; he had left Earth as a very young boy. Surely this serene and uncrowded Sarai offered more than poor tortured ant-heap Earth gave even to her overlords. And yet some mornings he woke up with the temple bells of Kyoto still chiming in his ears.

He stopped at the gate. "Will you honor my home for a cup of tea?" he asked.

"No, thanks," said Umfando, almost roughly. "You've a family to . . . to say goodbye to. I will see you when—"

Fire streaked across the sky. For an instant Il-Khan himself was lost in blue flame. The bolide struck somewhere among the mountains. A sheet of outraged energy flared above ragged peaks. Then smoke and dust swirled up like a devil, and moments afterward thunder came banging down through the valley.

Umfando whistled. "That was a monster!"

"A . . . yes . . . most unusual . . . yes, yes." Nakamura stammered something, somehow he bowed goodnight and somehow he kept from running along the path to his roof. But as he walked, he began to shake.

It was only a meteorite, he told himself frantically.

Only a meteorite. The space around a triple system like 40 Eridani, and especially around its biggest planet, was certain to be full of cosmic junk. Billions of stones hit Sarai every day. Hundreds of them got through to the surface. But Sarai was as big as Earth, he told himself. Sarai had oceans, deserts, uninhabited plains and forests . . . why, you were more likely to be killed by lightning than by a meteorite and—and—

Oh, the jewel in the lotus! he cried out. *I am afraid. I am afraid of the black sun.*

4

IT WAS RAINING AGAIN, but no one on Krasna pays
attention to that. They wear a few light nonabsorbent
garments and welcome the wetness on their bodies, a
moment's relief from saturated hot air. The clouds
thin overhead, so that the land glimmers with watery
brightness; sometimes the uppermost veils break
apart and Tau Ceti spears a blinding reddish shaft
through smoke-blue masses and silvery rain.

Chang Sverdlov rode into Dynamogorsk with a
hornbeast lashed behind his saddle. It had been a
dangerous chase, through the tidal marshes and up
over the bleak heights of Czar Nicholas IV Range,
but he needed evidence to back his story, that he had
only been going out to hunt. Mukerji, the chief in-
telligence officer of the Protectorate garrison, was
getting suspicious, God rot his brain.

Two soldiers came along the elevated sidewalk. Rain drummed on their helmets and sluiced off the slung rifles. Earth soldiers went in armed pairs on a street like Trumpet Road: for a Krasnan swamp-rancher, fisher, miner, logger, trapper, brawling away his accumulated loneliness, with a skinful of vodka or rice wine, a fluff-headed *fille-de-joie* to impress, and a sullen suspicion that the dice had been loaded, was apt to unlimber his weapons when he saw a blueback.

Sverdlov contented himself with spitting at their boots, which were about level with his head. It went unnoticed in the downpour. And in the noise, and crowding, and blinking lights, with thunder above the city's gables. He clucked to his saurian and guided her toward the middle of the slough called Trumpet Road. Its excitement lifted his anger a bit. *I'll report in,* he told himself, *and go wheedle an advance from the Guild bank, and then make up six weeks of bushranging in a way the joyhouses will remember!*

He turned off on the Avenue of Tigers and stopped before a certain inn. Tethering his lizard and throwing the guard a coin, he entered the taproom. It was as full of men and racket as usual. He shouldered up to the bar. The landlord recognized him; Sverdlov was a big and solid young man, bullet-headed, crop-haired, with a thick nose and small brown eyes in a pockmarked face. The landlord drew a mug of kvass, spiked it with vodka, and set it out. He nodded toward the ceiling. "I will tell her you are here," he said, and left.

Sverdlov leaned on the bar, one hand resting on a pistol butt, the other holding up his drink. *I could wish it really were one of the upstairs girls expecting me,* he thought. *Do we need all this melodrama of codes, countersigns, and cell organization?* He considered the seething of near-naked men in the room.

A chess game, a card game, a dirty joke, an Indian wrestling match, a brag, a wheedle, an incipient fight: his own Krasnans! It hardly seemed possible that any of those ears could have been hired by the Protector, and yet . . .

The landlord came back. "She's here and ready for you," he grinned. A couple of nearby men guffawed coarsely. Sverdlov tossed off his drink, lit one of the cheap cigars he favored, and pushed through to the stairs.

At the end of a third-floor corridor he rapped on a door. A voice invited him in. The room beyond was small and drably furnished, but its window looked down a straight street to the town's end and a sudden feathery splendor of rainbow trees. Lightning flimmered through the bright rain of Krasna. Sverdlov wondered scornfully if Earth had jungle and infinite promise on any doorstep.

He closed the door and nodded at the two men who sat waiting. He knew fat Li-Tsung; the gaunt Arabic-looking fellow was strange to him, and neither asked for an introduction.

Li-Tsung raised an eyebrow. Sverdlov said, "It is going well. They were having some new troubles—the aerospores were playing merry hell with the electrical insulation—but I think I worked out a solution. The Wetlanders are keeping our boys amply fed, and see no indication anyone has betrayed them. Yet."

The thin man asked, "This is the clandestine bomb factory?"

"No," said Li-Tsung. "It is time you learned of these matters, especially when you are leaving the system today. This man has been helping direct something more important than small-arms manufacture. They are tooling up out there to make interplanetary missiles."

"What for?" answered the stranger. "Once the

Fellowship has seized the mattercaster, it will be years before reinforcements can arrive from any other system. You'll have plenty of time to build heavy armament then.'' He glanced inquiringly at Sverdlov. Li-Tsung nodded. "In fact," said the thin man, "my division is trying to so organize things that there will be no closer Protectorate forces than Earth itself. Simultaneous revolution on a dozen planets. Then it would be at least two decades before spaceships could reach Tau Ceti."

"Ah," grunted Sverdlov. He lowered his hairy body into a chair. His cigar jabbed at the thin man. "Have you ever thought, the Earthlings are no fools? The mattercaster for the Tau Ceti System is up on Moon Two. Sure. We seize it, or destroy it. But is it the *only* transceiver around?"

The thin man choked. Li-Tsung murmured, "This is not for the rank and file. There is enough awe of Earth already, to hold the people back. But in point of fact, the Protector is an idiot if he has not picked at least one asteroid in some unlikely orbit, with a heavy-duty 'caster mounted on it. We can expect the Navy in our skies within hours of the independence proclamation. We must be prepared to fight!"

"But—" said the thin man, "but this means it will take years more to make ready than I thought. I had hoped—"

"The Centaurians rebelled prematurely, forty years ago," said Li-Tsung. "Let us never forget the lesson. Do you want to be lobotomized?"

Silence reigned for a while. Rain hammered on the roof. Down in the street, a couple of rangers just in from the Uplands were organizing an impromptu saurian fight.

"Well," said Sverdlov at last. "I'd better not stay here."

"Oh, but you should," said Li-Tsung. "You are supposedly visiting a woman, do you remember?"

Sverdlov snorted impatience, but reached for the little chess set in his pouch. "Who'll play me a quick game, then?"

"Are the bright lights that attractive?" asked Li-Tsung.

Sverdlov spoke an obscenity. "I've spent nearly my whole leave chasing through the bush and up into the Czar," he said. "I'll be off to Thovo—or worse yet, to Krimchak or Cupra or the Belt; Thovo has a settlement at least—for weeks. Months perhaps! Let me relax a little first."

"As a matter of fact," said Li-Tsung, "your next berth has already been assigned, and it is not to any of those places. It is outsystem." In his public *persona,* he was a minor official in the local branch of the Astronautical Guild.

"What?" Sverdlov cursed for a steady minute. "You mean I'm to be locked up for a month on some stinking ship in the middle of interstellar space, and—"

"Calmly, please, calmly. You won't be standing a routine single-handed just-in-case watch. This will be rather more interesting. You will be on the XA463, the *Southern Cross.*"

Sverdlov considered. He had taken his turn on the stellar vessels, but had no interest in them: they were a chore, one of the less desirable aspects of a spaceman's life. He had even been on duty when a new system was entered, but it had thrilled him not. Its planets turned out to be poisonous hells; he had finished his hitch and gone home before they completed the transceiver station. The devil could drink his share of the dedication party.

"I don't know which of them that would be," he said.

"It is bound for Alpha Crucis. Or was. Several years ago, the photographs taken by its instruments were routinely robo-analyzed on Earth. There were discrepancies. Chiefly, some of the background stars were displaced, the Einstein effect of mass on light rays. A more careful study revealed a feeble source of long radio waves in that direction. They appear to be the dying gasp of a star.''

Since Sverdlov's work involved him with the atomic nucleus, he could not help arguing: "I don't think so. The dying gasp, as you put it, would be gravitational potential energy, released as radiation when a star's own fires are exhausted. But a thing so cold it only emits in the far radio frequencies . . . I'd say that was merely some kind of turbulence in what passes for an atmosphere. That the star isn't just dying, it's *dead.*''

"I don't know," shrugged Li-Tsung. "Perhaps no one does. This expedition will be to answer such questions. They gave up on Alpha Crucis for the time being and decelerated the ship toward this black star. It is arriving there now. The next personnel will take up an orbit and make the initial studies. You are the engineer.''

Sverdlov drew heavily on his cigar. "Why me?" he protested. "I'm an interplanetary man. Except for those damned interstellar tours, I've never been out of the Tau Ceti System.''

"That may be one reason you were picked," said Li-Tsung. "The Guild does not like its men too provincial in outlook.''

"Surely," sneered Sverdlov. "We colonials can travel anywhere we please, except to Earth. Only our goods go to Earth without special permission.''

"You need not recruit us into the Fellowship of Independence," said the thin man in a parched voice.

Sverdlov clamped teeth together and got out through stiff lips: "There will be Earthlings aboard, won't there? It's asking for trouble, to put me on the same ship as an Earthling.''

"You will be very polite and cooperative," said Li-

Tsung sharply. "We have other reasons for your assignment. I cannot say much, but you can guess that we have sympathizers, even members, in the Guild . . . on a higher level than spacehand! It is possible that something of potential military value will be learned from the dark star. Who knows? Something about force fields or— Use your own imagination. It can do no harm to have a Fellowship man on the *Cross*. It may do some good. You will report to me when you return."

"Very well, very well," grumbled Sverdlov. "I can stand a month or two of Earthlings, I suppose."

"You will get your official orders soon," Li-Tsung told him. He glanced at his watch. "I think you can run along now; you have a reputation as a, hm-m, fast worker. Enjoy yourself."

"And don't get talking drunk," said the thin man.

Sverdlov paused in the doorway. "I don't," he said. "I wouldn't be still alive if I did."

5

THE AUTHORITY BOOKED first-class passages for expeditionary personnel, which in the case of a hop up to the Moon meant a direct ferry traveling at one gee all the way. Standing by the observation window, an untasted drink in his hand, David Ryerson remarked: "You know, this is only the third time I've ever been off Earth. And the other two, we transshipped at Satellite and went free-fall most of the trip."

"Sounds like fun," said Maclaren. "I must try it sometime."

"You . . . in your line of work . . . you must go to the Moon quite often," said Ryerson shyly.

Maclaren nodded. "Mount Ambartsumian Observatory, on Farside. Still a little dust and gas to bother us, of course, but I'll let the purists go out to Pluto Satellite and bring me back their plates."

"And . . . No. Forgive me." Ryerson shook his blond head.

"Go on." Maclaren, seated in a voluptuous form-fit lounger, offered a box of cigarets. He thought he knew Ryerson's type, serious, gifted, ambitious, but awe-smitten at the gimcrack fact of someone's hereditary technic rank. "Go ahead," he invited. "I don't embarrass easy."

"I was only wondering . . . who paid for your trips . . . the observatory or—"

"Great ancestors! The observatory!" Maclaren threw back his head and laughed with the heartiness of a man who had never had to be cautious. It rang above the low music and cultivated chatter; the ecdysiast paused an instant on her stage.

"My dear old colleague," said Maclaren, "I not only pay my own freight, I am expected to contribute generously toward the expenses of the institution. At least," he added, "my father is. But where else would money for pure research come from? You can't tax it out of the lower commons, y' know. They haven't got it. The upper commons are already taxed to the limit, short of pushing them back down into the hand-to-mouth masses. And the Protectorate rests on a technic class serving but not paying. That's the theory, anyhow: in practice, of course, a lot of 'em do neither. But how else would you support abstract science, except by patronage? Thank the Powers for the human snob instinct. It keeps both research and art alive."

Ryerson looked alarmed, glanced about as if expecting momentary arrest, finally lowered himself to the edge of a chair and almost whispered: "Yes, sir, yes, I know, naturally. I was just not so . . . so familiar with the details of . . . financing."

"Eh? But how could you have missed learning? You trained to be a scientist, didn't you?"

Ryerson stared out at Earth, sprawling splendor

across the constellations. "I set out to be a spaceman," he said, blushing. "But in the last couple of years I got more interested in tachyonics, had to concentrate too much on catching up in that field to . . . well . . . also, I was planning to emigrate, so I wasn't interested in— The colonies need trained men. The opportunities—"

Pioneering is an unlimited chance to become the biggest frog, provided the puddle is small enough, thought Maclaren. But he asked aloud, politely, "Where to?"

"Rama. The third planet of Washington 5584."

"Hm? Oh, yes. The new one, the GO dwarf. Uh, how far from here?"

"Ninety-seven light years. Rama has just passed the five-year survey test." Ryerson leaned forward, losing shyness in his enthusiasm. "Actually, sir, Rama is the most nearly terrestroid planet they have yet found. The biochemistry is so similar to Earth's that one can even eat many of the native plants. Oh, and there are climatic zones, oceans, forests, mountains, a single big moon—"

"And thirty years of isolation," said Maclaren. "Nothing connecting you to the universe but a voice."

Ryerson reddened again. "Does that matter so much?" he asked aggressively. "Are we losing a great deal by that?"

"I suppose not," said Maclaren. *Your lives, perhaps,* he thought. *Remember the Shadow Plague on New Kashmir? Or your children—the mutation virus on Gondwana. Five years is not long enough to learn a planet; the thirty-year quarantine is an arbitrary minimum. And, of course, one finds the more obvious and spectacular things, which merely kill colonists without threatening the human race. Storms, quakes, morasses, volcanoes, meteorites. Cumulative poisoning. Wild animals. Unsuspected half-intelligent aborigines. Strangeness, loneliness, madness. It's no wonder the colonies which survive develop their own cultures. It's no wonder they come to think of Earth as a parasite on their own tedious heroisms. Of course, with ten billion people, and a great deal of once arable country sterilized by radiation, Earth has little choice.*

What I would like to know is, why does anyone emigrate in the first place? The lessons are ghastly enough; why do otherwise sensible people, like this boy, refuse to learn them?

"Oh, well," he said aloud. He signaled the waiter. "Refuel us, chop-chop."

Ryerson looked in some awe at the chit which the other man thumbprinted. He could not suppress it: "Do you always travel first class to the Moon?"

Maclaren put a fresh cigaret between his lips and touched his lighter-ring to the end. His smile cocked it at a wry angle. "I suppose," he answered, "I have always traveled first class through life."

The ferry made turnover without spilling a drink or a passenger and backed down onto Tycho Port. Maclaren adjusted without a thought to Lunar gravity, Ryerson turned a little green and swallowed a pill. But even in his momentary distress, the younger man was bewildered at merely walking through a tube to a monorail station. Third-class passengers must submit to interminable official bullying: safety regulations, queues, assignment to hostel. Now, within minutes, he was again on soft cushions, staring through crystalline panes at the saw-toothed magnificence of mountains.

When the train got under way, he gripped his hands together, irrationally afraid. It took him a while to hunt down the reason: the ghost of his father's God, ranting at pride and sloth from the tomb which the son had erected.

"Let's eat," said Maclaren. "I chose this train with malice aforethought. It's slow; we can enjoy our meal en route, and the chef puts his heart into the oysters won-ton."

"I'm not . . . not hungry," stammered Ryerson.

Maclaren's dark, hooked face flashed a grin. "That's what cocktails and hors d'oeuvres are for, lad. Stuff yourself. If it's true what I've heard of deep-space rations, we're in for a dreary month or two."

"You mean you've never been on an interstellar ship?"

"Of course not. Never been beyond the Moon in my life. Why should I do any such ridiculous thing?"

Maclaren's cloak swirled like fire as he led the way toward the diner. Beneath an iridescent white tunic, his legs showed muscular and hairless, down to the tooled-leather buskins; the slant of the beret on his head was pure insolence. Ryerson, trailing drably behind in a spaceman's gray coverall, felt bitterness. *What the hell have I been dragged away from Tamara for? Does this peacock know a mass from a scroll in the ground? He's hired himself a toy, is all, because for a while he's bored with wine and women . . . and Tamara is locked away on a rock with a self-righteous old beast who hates the sound of her name!*

As they sat down at their table, Maclaren went on: "But this is too good a chance to pass up. I found me a tame mathematician last year and sicced him onto the Schrödinger equation—Sugimoto's relativistic version, I mean; Yuen postulates too bloody much for my taste—anyhow, he worked it out for the quantities involved in a dark star too small to form a black hole, mass and gravitational intensities and cetera, a body so old that it's used up its last potential energies. His results make us both wonder if it doesn't go past the neutron star stage of degeneracy, to something entirely new to us, at least at the core. One gigantic quark? Well, maybe that's excessively fantastic. But consider—''

And while the monorail ran on toward Farside, Maclaren left the Interhuman language quite behind him. Ryerson could follow tensors, even when scribbled on a menu, but Maclaren had some new function, symbolized by a pneumatic female outline, that *reduced* to a generalized tensor under certain conditions. Ryerson stepped out on Farside, two hours later, with his brain rotating.

He had heard of the cyclopean installations which fill the whole of Yukawa Crater and spread out onto the plains beyond. Who has not? But all he saw on this first visit was a gigantic concourse, a long slideway tunnel, and a good many uniformed technicians. He made some timid mention of his disappointment to Maclaren. The New Zealander nodded: "Exactly. There's more romance, more sense of distance covered, and a devil of a lot better scenery, in an afternoon on the bay, than in a fifty-light-year leap. I say space travel is overrated. And it's a fact, I've heard, that spacemen themselves prefer the interplanetary runs. They take the dull interstellar watches as a matter of duty, by turns.''

Here and there the tunnel branched off, signs indicating the way to Alpha Centauri Jump, Tau Ceti Jump, 40 Eridani Jump, all the long-colonized systems. Those were for passengers; freight went by other beams. No great bustle filled any of the tubes. Comparatively few Earthlings had occasion to visit outsystem on business, still fewer could afford it for pleasure, and of course no colonial came here without a grudging okay. The Protector had trouble enough; he was not going to expose the mother planet and its restless billions to new ideas born under new skies, nor let any more colonials than he could help see first-hand what an inferior position

they held. That was the real reason for the ban; every
educated Terrestrial knew as much. The masses,
being illiterate, swallowed a vague official excuse
about trade policy.

The branches leading to Sirius Jump, Procyon
Jump, and the other attained but uncolonizable
systems, were almost deserted. Little came from such
places—perhaps an occasional gem or exotic
chemical. But relay stations had been established
there, for 'casting to more useful planets.

Ryerson's heart leaped when he passed a newly activated sign: an arrow and WASHINGTON 5584 JUMP
burning above. *That* tunnel would be filled, come
next week!

He should have been in the line. And Tamara.
Well, there would be later waves. His passage already
paid for, he had had no difficulty about transferring
to another section.

To make conversation, he said through a tightness:
"Where are the bulkheads?"

"Which ones?" asked Maclaren absently.

"Safety bulkheads. A receiver does fail once in a
great while, you know. That's why the installations
here are spread out so much, why every star has a
separate 'caster. You get a vast amount of energy involved in each transmission—one reason why a
'casting is more expensive than transportation by
spaceship. Even a small increment, undissipated, can
melt a whole chamber."

"Oh, yes. That." Maclaren had let Ryerson wax
pompous about the obvious because it was plain he
needed something to bolster himself. What itched the
kid, anyhow? One should think that when the
Authority offered a fledgling a post on an expedition
as fundamental as this— Of course, it had upset
Ryerson's plans of emigration. But not importantly.
There was no danger he would find all the choice sites
on Rama occupied if he came several weeks late: too

few people had the fare as it was.

Maclaren said, "I see what you mean. Yes, the bulkheads are there, but recessed into the walls and camouflaged. You don't want to emphasize possible danger to the cash customers, eh? Some technic might get annoyed and make trouble."

"Some day," said Ryerson, "they'll reduce the energy margin needed; and they'll figure how to reproduce a Frank tube, rather than manufacture it. Record the pattern and recreate from a matter bank. Then anyone can afford to ride the beams. Interplanetary ships, yes, air and surface craft, will become obsolete."

Maclaren made no answer. He had sometimes thought, more or less idly, about the unrealized potentialities of mattercasting. Hard to say whether personal immortality would be a good thing or not. Not for the masses, surely! Too many of them as it was. But a select few, like Terangi Maclaren—or was it worth the trouble? Even given boats, chess, music, the Nō Drama, beautiful women and beautiful spectroscopes, life could get heavy.

As for matter transmission, the difficulty and hence the expense lay in the complexity of the signal. Consider an adult human. He has some 10^{14} cells in him, each an elaborate structure involving many proteins with molecular weights in the millions. You had to scan every one of those molecules—identify it structurally, ticket its momentary energy levels, and place it in proper spatiotemporal relationship to every other molecule—as nearly simultaneously as the laws of physics permitted. You couldn't take a man apart, or·reassemble him, in more than a few microseconds; he wouldn't survive it. You couldn't transmit a recognizable beefsteak in much less of a hurry.

So the scanning beam went through and through,

like a blade of energy. It touched every atom in its path, was modified thereby, and flashed that modification onto the transmitter matrix. But such fury destroyed. The scanned object was reduced to gas, so quickly that only an oscilloscope could watch the process. The gas was sucked into the destructor chamber and atomically condensed in the matter bank; in time it would become an incoming passenger, or incoming freight. In a sense, the man had died.

If you could record the signal which entered the transmitter matrix, you could keep such a record indefinitely, recreate the man and his instantaneous memories, thoughts, habits, prejudices, hopes and loves and hates and horrors, a thousand years afterward. You could create a billion identical men. Or, more practically, a single handmade prototype could become a billion indistinguishable copies; nothing would be worth more than any load of dirt. Or . . . superimpose the neurone trace-patterns, memories, of a lifetime, onto a recorded twenty-year-old body, be born again and live forever!

The signal was too complex, though. An unpromising research program went on. Perhaps in a few centuries they would find some trick which would enable them to record a man, or just a Frank tube. Meanwhile, transmission had to be simultaneous with scanning. The signal went out. Probably it would be relayed a few times. Eventually the desired receiving chamber got it. The receiver matrix, powered by dying atomic nuclei, flung gases together, formed higher elements, formed molecules and cells and dreams according to the signal, in microseconds. It was designed as an energy-consuming process, for obvious reasons: packing fraction energy was dissipated in nuclear and magnetic fields, to help shape the man (or the beefsteak, or the spaceship, or the colonial planet's produce). He left the receiving chamber and went about his business.

A mono-isotopic element is a simple enough signal to record, Maclaren reminded himself, *though even that requires a houseful of transistor elements. So this civilization can afford to be extravagant with metals—can use pure mercury as the raw material of a spaceship's blast, for instance. But we still eat our bread in the sweat of some commoner's brow.*

Not for the first time, but with no great indignation—life was too short for anything but amusement at the human race—Maclaren wondered if the recording problem really was as difficult as the physicists claimed. No government likes revolutions, and molecular duplication would revolutionize society beyond imagining. Just think how they had to guard the stations as it was, and stick them out here on the Moon . . . otherwise some fanatic might steal a tube of radium from a hospital and duplicate enough to sterilize a planet!

"Oh, well," he said, half aloud.

They reached the special exploratory section and entered an office where they found red tape to unsnarl. Ryerson let Maclaren handle it, and spent the time trying to understand that soon the pattern which was himself would be embodied in newly shaped atoms, a hundred light-years from Tamara. The idea wouldn't penetrate. It was only words.

Finally the papers were stamped. The transceivers to/from an interstellar spaceship could handle several hundred kilos at a time; Maclaren and Ryerson went together. They had a moment's wait because of locked safety switches on the *Southern Cross:* someone else was arriving or departing ahead of them.

"Watch that first step," said Maclaren. "It's a honey."

"What?" Ryerson blinked at him, uncomprehending.

The circuit closed. The pair felt no sensation, the process went too fast.

The scanner put its signal into the matrix. Inconceivable energies surged within a thermonuclear fire chamber; nothing controlled them, nothing could control them, but the force fields they themselves generated. Matter pulsed in and out of existence *qua* matter, from particle to gamma ray quantum and back. Since quanta have no rest mass, the pulsations disturbed the geometry of space according to the laws of Einsteinian mechanics. Gravitational waves laid hold of the tachyons which sprang into being, paired with tardyons, and formed them into a beam, and modulated it.

At hundreds of times the speed of light, the beam departed Luna, bearing the unimaginably complex signal which corresponded to two human beings. Distance attenuated it, but small, automated stations planted along the way relayed, and eventually refined its aim. After minutes, the tachyon pattern found and activated a matrix aboard the *Cross*.

Despite the pill inside him, Ryerson felt as if the bottom had dropped out of the world. He grabbed for a handhold. The after-image of the transmitter chamber yielded to the coils and banks of the receiver room on a spaceship. He hung weightless, a thousand billion billion kilometers from Earth.

6

Forward of the 'casting chambers, "above" them during acceleration, were fuel deck, gyros, and air-renewal plant. Then you passed through the observation deck, where instruments and laboratory equipment crowded together. A flimsy wall around the shaftway marked off the living quarters: folding bunks, galley, bath, table, benches, shelves, lockers, all crammed into a six-meter circle.

Seiichi Nakamura wrapped one leg casually around a stanchion, to keep himself from drifting in air currents, and made a ceremony out of leafing through the log book in his hands. It gave the others a chance to calm down, and the yellow-haired boy, David Ryerson, seemed to need it. The astrophysicist, Maclaren, achieved the unusual feat of lounging in free fall; he puffed an expensive

Earthside cigaret and wrinkled his patrician nose at the pervading smell of an old ship, two hundred years of cooking and sweat and machine oil. The big, ugly young engineer, Sverdlov, merely looked sullen. Nakamura had never met any of them before.

"Well, gentlemen," he said at last. "Pardon me, I had to check the data recorded by the last pilot. Now I know approximately where we are at." He laughed with polite self-deprecation. "Of course you are familiar with the articles. The pilot is captain. His duty is to guide the ship where the chief scientist—Dr. Maclaren-san in this case—wishes, within the limits of safety as determined by his own judgment. In case of my death or disability, command devolves upon the engineer, ah, Sverdlov-san, and you are to return home as soon as practicable. Yes-s-s. But I am sure we will have a most pleasant and instructive expedition together."

He felt the banality of his words. It was the law, and a wise one, that authority be defined at once if non-Guild personnel were aboard. Some pilots contented themselves with reading the regulations aloud, but it had always seemed an unnecessarily cold procedure to Nakamura. Only . . . he saw a sick bewilderment in Ryerson's eyes, supercilious humor in Maclaren's, angry impatience in Sverdlov's . . . his attempt at friendliness had gone flat.

"We do not operate so formally," he went on in a lame fashion. "We shall post a schedule of housekeeping duties and help each other, yes? Well. That is for later. Now as to the star, we have approximate date and estimates taken by previous watches. It appears to have about twice the mass of Sol. That must have been one fantastic supernova explosion, blowing away nearly the whole of a giant star, no? Perhaps the original composition was unusual—but this is not my field of knowledge. The radius is hardly more than Earth's, quite possibly less. It emits detectably only in the lower radio frequencies, and that is feeble. I have here a quick reading of the spectrum which may interest you, Dr. Maclaren.''

The big dark man reached for it. His brows went up. "Now this," he said, "is the weirdest collection of wavelengths I ever saw." He flickered experienced eyes along the column of numbers. "Seems to be a lot of triplets, but the lines are so broad, judging from the probable errors given, that I can't be sure without more careful—hm-m." Glancing back at Nakamura: "Whereabouts are we with relation to the star?"

"Approximately two million kilometers from its center of mass. We are being drawn toward it, of course, since an orbit has not yet been established, but have ample radial velocity of our own to—"

"Never mind." The sophistication dropped from Maclaren like a tunic. He said with a boy's eagerness, "I want to get as near the star as possible. How close do you think you can put us?"

Nakamura smiled. He had a feeling Maclaren could prove likeable. "Too close isn't prudent. We could encounter meteoroids."

"Not around this one!" exclaimed Maclaren. "You yourself said it. If physical theory is anything but mescaline dreams, this kind of dead star is the clinker of a supernova. Any matter orbiting in its neighborhood became incandescent gas long ago."

"Atmosphere?" asked Nakamura dubiously. "Since we have nothing to see by, except starlight, we could hit its air."

"Hm. Yes. I suppose it would have some. But not very deep: too compressed to be deep. In fact, the radio photosphere, from which the previous watches estimated the star's diameter, must be nearly identical with the fringes of atmosphere."

"It would also take a great deal of reaction mass to

pull us back out of its attraction, if we got too close," said Nakamura. He unclipped the calculator at his belt and made a few quick computations. "In fact, this vessel cannot escape from a distance much less than three-quarters million kilometers, if we are to have a reasonable amount of mass left for maneuvering around afterward. And I am sure you wish to explore regions farther from the star, yes-s-s? However, I am willing to go that close."

Maclaren smiled. "Good enough. How long to arrive?"

"I estimate three hours, including time to establish the orbit." Nakamura looked around at their faces. "If everyone is prepared to go on duty, it is best we get into the desired path at once."

"Not even a cup of tea first?" grumbled Sverdlov.

Nakamura nodded at Maclaren and Ryerson. "You gentlemen will please prepare tea and sandwiches, and take them to the engineer and myself in about ninety minutes."

"Now, wait!" protested Maclaren. "We've hardly arrived. I haven't so much as looked at my instruments. I have to set up—"

"In ninety minutes, if you will be so kind. Very well, let us assume our posts."

Nakamura turned from Maclaren's suddenly mutinous look and Sverdlov's broad grin. He entered the shaftway and pulled himself along it by the rungs. Through the transparent plastic he saw the observation deck fall behind. The boat deck was next, heavy storage levels followed, and then he was forward, into the main turret.

It was a clear plastic bubble, unshuttered now when the sole outside illumination was a wintry blaze of stars. Floating toward the controls, Nakamura grew aware of the silence. So quiet. So uncountably many stars. The constellations were noticeably distorted, some altogether foreign, in a crystal darkness. No use looking for Sol without a telescope, here on the lonely edge of the known.

Fear of raw emptiness lay tightly coiled within him. He smothered it by routine: strapped himself before the console, checked the instruments one by one, spoke with Sverdlov down the length of the ship. His fingers chattered out a computation on a set of keys, he fed the tape to the robot, he felt a faint tug as the gyros woke up, swiveling the vessel into position for blast. Even now, at the end of acceleration to half light-speed and deceleration to a few hundred kilometers per second, the *Cross* bore several tons of reaction-mass mercury. The total mass, including hull, equipment, and payload, was a bit over one kiloton. Accordingly, her gyroscopes needed half an hour to turn her completely around.

Waiting, he studied the viewscreens. Since he must back down on his goal, what they showed him was more important than what his eyes saw through this turret in the nose. He could not make out the black sun. *Well, what do you expect?* he asked himself angrily. *It must be occulting a few stars, but there are too many.* "Dr. Maclaren," he said into the intercom, "can you give me a radio directional on the target, as a check?"

"Aye, aye." A surly answer. Maclaren resented having to put his toys to work. He would rather have been taking spectra, reading ionoscopes, gulping gas and dust samples from outside into his analyzers, every centimeter of the way. Well, he would just have to get those data when they receded from the star again.

Nakamura's eyes strayed down the ship herself, as shown in the viewscreens. *Old,* he thought. *The very nation which built her has ceased to exist. But good work. A man's work outlives his hands. Though what remains of the little ivory figures my father carved to ornament our house? What chance did my brother have to create, before he shriveled in my arms? No!* He shut off the thought, like a surgeon clamping a vein, and refreshed his memory of the *Cygnus* class.

This hull was a sphere of reinforced self-sealing plastic, fifty meters across, its outside smoothness broken by hatches, ports, airlocks, and the like. Most prominent were the ionizing lasers and the generators of magnetohydrodynamic fields, which warded off the interstellar gas that would otherwise, at high speeds, have filled the ship with lethal radiation. Various decks sliced the hull in parallel planes. Aft, diametrically opposite this turret, it opened on the fire chamber. And thence ran two thin metal skeletons, thirty meters apart, a hundred meters long, like radio masts or ancient oil derricks. They comprised two series of rings, a couple of centimeters in diameter, with auxiliary wiring and a spidery framework holding it all together—the ion accelerators, built into and supported by the tachyonic transceiver web.

"A ten-second blast, if you please, Engineer Sverdlov," said Nakamura.

The instruments showed him a certain unbalance in the distribution of mass within the hull. Yussuf bin Suleiman, who had lately finished watch aboard the ship and gone back to Earth, was sloppy about . . . no, it was unjust to think so . . . say that he had his own style of piloting. Nakamura set the pumps to work. Mercury ran from the fuel decks to the trim tanks.

By then the vessel was pointed correctly and it was time to start decelerating again. "Stand by for blast. . . . Report. . . . I shall want one-point-five-seven standard gees for—" Nakamura reeled it off almost automatically.

It rumbled in the ship. Weight came, like a sudden fist in the belly. Nakamura held his body relaxed in

harness, only his eyes moved, now and then a finger
touched a control. The main computer did nearly
everything, through its sensor-effector systems and
flexibly programmed light-speed calculations. His
part was, basically, to make its decisions for it. For
this, he must well-nigh merge his being with
readouts, meters, switches, verniers, make himself
one with his vessel. That was the core of judo, of life,
to lose the part within the whole and thereby become
the whole—on a practical level, to keep every part of
the organism at ease except those precise tissues
needed for the moment's task. Why was it so dam-
nably difficult to put into practice?

Mercury fed through pipes and pumps, past Sverdlov's control board, past the radiation wall, into the
expansion chamber and through the ionizer and so as
a spray past the sunlike heart of a thermonuclear
plasma. Briefly, each atom endured a rage of
energies. It broke down, underwent a cascade of
nucleon transformations, became proton-antiproton
pairs. Magnetic fields separated them as they were
born: positive and negative particles fled down the
linear accelerators. The plasma, converting the death
of matter directly to electricity, charged the rings at
successively higher potentials. When the particles
emerged from the last, they were traveling at three-
fourths the speed of light.

At such an exhaust velocity, no great mass need be
discharged. Nor was the twin stream visible; it was
too efficient. Sensitive instruments might have de-
tected a pale gamma-colored splotch, very far behind
the ship, as a few opposites finally converged on one
another, but that effect was of no importance.

The process was energy-eating. It had to be. Else
surplus heat would have vaporized the ship. The
plasma furnished energy and to spare. The process
was a good deal more complex than a few words can
describe, and yet less so than an engineer accustomed

to more primitive branches of his art might imagine.

Nakamura gave himself up to the instruments. Their readings checked out with his running computation. The *Cross* was approaching the black star in a complex spiral curve, the resultant of several velocities and two accelerating vectors, which would become a nearly circular orbit 750,000 kilometers out.

He started to awareness of time when young Ryerson came up the shaftway rungs. "Oh," he exclaimed.

"Tea, sir," said the boy shyly.

"Thank you. Ah . . . set it down there, please . . . the regulations forbid entering this turret during blast without inquiring of the— No, no. Please!" Nakamura waved a hand, laughing. "You did not know. There is no harm done."

He saw Ryerson, stooped under one and a half gravities, lift a heavy head to the foreign stars. The Milky Way formed a cold halo about his tangled hair. Nakamura asked gently, "This is your first time in extrasolar space, yes?"

"Y-yes, sir." Ryerson licked his lips. The blue eyes were somehow hazy, unable to focus closer than the nebulae.

"Do not—" Nakamura paused. He had been about to say, "Do not be afraid," but it might hurt. He felt after words. "Space is a good place to meditate," he said. "I use the wrong word, of course. 'Meditation,' in Zen, consists more of an attempt at identification with the universe than verbalized thinking. What I mean to say," he floundered, "is this. Some people feel themselves so helplessly small out here that they become frightened. Others, remembering that home is no more than a step away through the transmitter, become careless and arrogant, the cosmos merely a set of meaningless numbers to them. Both attitudes

are wrong, and have killed men. But if you think of
yourself as being a *part* of everything else—in-
tegral—the same forces in you which shaped the
suns—do you see?''

" 'The heavens declare the glory of God,' "
whispered Ryerson, " 'and the firmament showeth
His handiwork'. . . . It is a terrible thing to fall into
the hands of the living God.''

He had not been listening, and Nakamura did not
understand English. The pilot sighed. "I think you
had best return to the observation deck," he said.
"Dr. Maclaren may have need of you."

Ryerson nodded mutely and went back down the
shaft.

I preach a good theory, Nakamura told himself.
*Why can I not practice it? Because a stone fell from
heaven onto Sarai, and suddenly father and mother
and sister and house were not. Because Hideki died in
my arms, after the universe had casually tortured
him. Because I shall never see Kyoto again, where
every morning was full of cool bells. Because I am a
slave of myself.*

And yet, he thought, *sometimes I have achieved
peace. And only in space.*

Now he saw the dead sun through a viewscreen,
when his ship swung so that it transmitted the Milky
Way. It was a tiny blackness. The next time around,
it had grown. He wondered if it was indeed blacker
than the sky. Nonsense. It should reflect starlight,
should it not? But what color was metallic hydrogen?
What gases overlay the metal? Space, especially here,
was not absolutely black: a thin but measurable
nebular cloud lay around the star. So conceivably the
star might be blacker than the sky.

"I must ask Maclaren," he murmured to himself.
"He can measure it, very simply, and tell me.
Meditation upon the concept of blacker than total

blackness is not helpful, it seems.'' That brought him a wry humor, which untensed his muscles. He grew aware of weariness. It should not have been; he had only been sitting here and pressing controls. He poured a cup of scalding tea and drank noisily and gratefully.

Down and down. Nakamura fell into an almost detached state. Now the star was close, not much smaller than the Moon seen from Earth. It grew rapidly, and crawled still more rapidly around the circle of the viewscreens. Now it was as big as Batu, at closest approach to Sarai. Now it was bigger. The rhythms entered Nakamura's blood. Dimly, he felt himself join with the ship, the fields, the immense interplay of forces. And this was why he went again and yet again into space. He touched the manual controls, assisting the robots, correcting, revising, in a pattern of unformulated but bodily known harmonies, a dance, a dream, yielding, controlling, unselfness, Nirvana, peace and wholeness. . . .

Fire!

The shock rammed Nakamura's spine against his skull. He felt his teeth clashed together. Blood from a bitten tongue welled in his mouth. Thunder roared between the walls.

He stared into the screens, clawing for comprehension. The ship was a million or so kilometers out. The black star was half a degree wide, snipped out of an unnamed alien constellation. The far end of the ion accelerator system was white hot. Even as Nakamura watched, the framework curled up, writhed like fingers in agony, and vaporized.

''*What's going on?*'' Horror bawled from the engine room.

The thrust fell off and weight dropped sickeningly. Nakamura saw hell eat along the accelerators. He jerked his eyes around to the primary megammeter.

Its needle sank down a tale of numbers. The four outermost rings were already destroyed. He saw the next one shrivel.

It could not be felt, but he knew how the star's vast hand clamped on the ship and reeled her inward.

Metal whiffed into space. Underloaded, the nuclear system howled its anger. Echoes banged between shivering decks.

"Cut!" cried Nakamura. His hand slapped the pilot's master switch.

The silence that fell, and the no-weight, were like death.

Someone's voice gabbled from the observation deck. Automatically, Nakamura chopped that interference out of the intercom circuit.

"Engineer Sverdlov," he called. "What happened? Do you know what is wrong?"

"No. No." A groan. But at least the man lived. "Somehow the—the ion streams . . . seem to have . . . gotten diverted. The focusing fields went awry. The blast struck the rings—but it couldn't happen!"

Nakamura hung on to his harness with all ten fingers. *I will not scream,* he shouted. *I will not scream.*

"The 'caster web seems to be gone too," said a machine using his throat. His brother's dead face swam among the stars, outside the turret, and mouthed at him.

"Aye." Sverdlov must be hunched over his own viewscreens. After a while that tingled, he said harshly: "Not yet beyond repair. All ships carry a few replacement parts, in case of meteoroids or— We can repair the web and transmit ourselves out of here."

"How long to do that job? Quickly!"

"How should I know?" A dragon snarl. Then: "I'd have to go out and take a closer look. The damaged sections will have to be cut away. It'll probably be necessary to machine some fittings. With luck, we can do it in several hours."

Nakamura paused. He worked his hands together, strength opposing strength; he drew slow breaths, rolled his head to loosen the neck muscles, finally closed his eyes and contemplated peace for as long as needful. And a measure of peace came. The death of this little ego was not so terrible after all, provided said ego refrained from wishing to hold Baby-san in its arms one more time.

Almost absently, he punched the keys of the general computer. It was no surprise to see his guess verified.

"Are you there?" called Sverdlov, as if across centuries.

"Yes. I beg your pardon. Several hours to repair the web, did you say? By that time, drifting free, we will have crashed on the star."

"What? But we're *in* orbit! Eccentric, maybe, but—"

"It is too narrow. We still have too much inward radial velocity. If the star were a single point, we would be in no danger; but it has volume. As nearly as I can determine—though there are so many uncertainties—our present orbit intersects the star. I think I can put us into a safe path before the whatever-it-is force has quite destroyed the accelerators. Yes."

"But you'll burn them up! And the web! We'll damage the web beyond repair!"

"Perhaps something can be improvised, once we are in orbit. But if we continue simply falling, we are dead men."

"No!" Almost, Sverdlov shrieked. "Listen, maybe we can repair the web in time. Maybe we'll only need a couple of hours for the job. There's a chance. But caught in an orbit, with the web melted or vaporized . . . do you know how to build one from raw metal? I don't!''

"We have a tachyonics specialist aboard. If anyone can fashion us a new transmitter, he can.''

"And if he can't, we're trapped out here! To starve! Better to crash and be done!''

Nakamura's hands began to dance over the keyboard. He demanded data of the instruments, calculations of the computers, and nothing of the autopilot. For no machine could help steer a vessel whose thrust-engine was being unpredictably devoured. This would be a manual task.

"I am the captain,'' he said, as mildly as possible.

"Not any more!''

Nakamura slapped his master switch. "You have now been cut out of the control circuits,'' he said. "Please remain at your post.'' He opened the intercom to the observation deck. "Will the two honorable scientists be so kind as to stop the engineer from interfering with the pilot?''

7

FOR A MOMENT, the rage in Chang Sverdlov was such that blackness flapped before his eyes.

When he regained himself, he found the view-screens still painted with ruin. Starlight lay wan along the frail network of the transceiver web and the two sets of rings which it held together. At the far end the metal glowed red. A few globs of spattered stuff orbited like lunatic fireflies. Beyond the twisted burned-off end of the system, light-years dropped away to the cold blue glitter of a thousand crowding stars. The dead sun was just discernible, a flattened darkness. It seemed to be swelling visibly. Whether that was a real effect or not, Sverdlov felt the dread of falling, the no-weight horrors, like a lump in his belly.

He hadn't been afraid of null-gee since he was a

child. In his cadet days, he had invented more pranks involving free fall than any two other boys. But he had never been cut off from home in this fashion. Krasna had never been more than an interplanetary flight or an interstellar Jump away.

And that cookbook pilot would starve out here to save his worthless ship?

Sverdlov unbuckled his harness. He kicked himself across the little control room, twisted among the pipes and wheels and dials of the fuel-feed section like a swimming fish, and came to the tool rack. He chose a long wrench and arrowed for the shaftway. His fury had chilled into resolution: *I don't want to kill him, but he'll have to be made to see reason. And quickly, or we really will crash!*

He was rounding the transmitter chamber when deceleration resumed. He had been going up by the usual process, grab a rung ahead of you and whip your weightless body beyond. Suddenly two Terrestrial gravities snatched him.

He closed fingers about one of the bars. His left arm straightened, with a hundred and ninety kilos behind. The hand tore loose. He let go the wrench and caught with his right arm, jamming it between a rung and the shaft wall. The impact smashed across his biceps. Then his left hand clawed fast and he hung. He heard the wrench skid past the gyro housing, hit a straight drop-off, and clang on the after radiation shield.

Gasping, he found a lower rung with his feet and sagged for a minute. The right arm was numb, until the pain woke in it. He flexed the fingers. Nothing broken.

But he was supposed to be in harness. Nakamura's maneuvers might demand spurts of ten or fifteen gravities, if the accelerators could still put out that much. The fear of being smeared across a bulkhead jolted into Sverdlov. He scrambled over the rungs. It was nightmarishly like climbing through glue. After a thousand years he burst into the living quarters.

Maclaren sat up in one of the bunks. "No further, please," he said.

The deceleration climbed a notch. His weight was iron on Sverdlov's shoulders. He started back into the shaft. "No!" cried Ryerson. But it was Maclaren who flung off bunk harness and climbed to the deck. The brown face gleamed wet, but Maclaren smiled and said: "Didn't you hear me?"

Sverdlov grunted and re-entered the shaft, both feet on a rung. *I can make it up to the bubble and get my hands on Nakamura's throat.* Maclaren stood for a gauging instant, as Sverdlov's foot crept toward the next rung. Finally the physicist added with a sneer in the tone: "When a technic says sit, you squat . . . colonial."

Sverdlov halted. "What was that?" he asked slowly.

"I can haul you out of there if I must, you backwoods pig," said Maclaren, "but I'd rather you came to me."

Sverdlov wondered, with an odd quick sadness, why he responded. Did an Earthling's yap make so much difference? He decided that Maclaren would probably make good on that promise to follow him up the shaft, and under this weight a fight on the rungs could kill them both. Therefore—Sverdlov's brain seemed as heavy as his bones. He climbed back and stood slumping on the observation deck. "Well?" he said.

Maclaren folded his arms. "Better get into a bunk," he advised.

Sverdlov lumbered toward him. In a shimmery wisp of tunic, the Earthling looked muscular enough, but he probably massed ten kilos less, and lacked several centimeters of the Krasnan's height and reach. A few swift blows would disable him, and it might still not be too late to stop Nakamura.

"Put up your fists," said Sverdlov hoarsely.

Maclaren unfolded his arms. A sleepy smile crossed his face. Sverdlov came in, swinging at the eagle beak. Maclaren's head moved aside. His hands came up, took Sverdlov's arm, and applied a cruel leverage. Sverdlov gasped, broke free by sheer strength, and threw a blow to the ribs. Maclaren stopped that fist with an edge-on chop at the wrist behind it; almost, Sverdlov thought he felt the bones crack. They stood toe to toe. Sverdlov drew back the other fist. Maclaren punched him in the groin. The Krasnan doubled over in a jag of anguish. Maclaren rabbit-punched him. Sverdlov went to one knee. Maclaren kicked him in the solar plexus. Sverdlov fell over and struck the floor with three gravities to help.

Through a wobbling, ringing darkness, he heard the Earthling: "Help me with this beef, Dave." And he felt himself dragged across the floor, somehow manhandled into a bunk and harnessed.

His mind returned. Pain stabbed and flickered through him. He struggled to sit up. "That was an Earthman way to fight," he pushed out through a swelling mouth.

"I don't enjoy fighting," said Maclaren from his own bunk, "so I got it over with as soon as possible."

"You—" The Krasnan lifted grotesquely heavy hands and fumbled with his harness. "I'm going to the control turret. If you try to stop me this time—"

"You're already too late, brother Sverdlov," said Maclaren coolly. "Whatever you were setting out to forestall has gone irrevocably far toward happening."

The words were a physical blow.

"It's . . . yes," said the engineer. "I'm too late."

The shout burst from him: "We're all too late, now!"

"Ease back," said Maclaren. "Frankly, your behavior doesn't give me much confidence in your judgment about anything."

It rumbled through the ship. That shouldn't be, thought Sverdlov's training; even full blast ought to be nearly noiseless, and this was only fractional. Sweat prickled his skin. For the first time in a violent life, he totally realized that he could die.

"I'm sorry for what I called you," said Maclaren. "I had to stop you, but now I apologize."

Sverdlov made no answer. He stared up at a blank ceiling. Oddly, his first emotion, as rage ebbed, was an overwhelming sorrow. He would never see Krasna made free.

8

SILENCE AND NO-WEIGHT were dreamlike. For a
reason obscure to himself, Maclaren had dimmed the
fluoros around the observation deck, so that twilight
filled it and the scientific apparatus crouched in racks
and on benches seemed to be a herd of long-necked
monsters. Thus there was nothing to drown the steely
brilliance of the stars, when you looked out an unshuttered port.

The star hurtled across his field of view. Her eccentric orbit took the *Cross* around it in 52 minutes.
Here, at closest approach, they were only half a
million kilometers away. The thing had the visual
diameter of one and a half full Moons. It was
curiously vague of outline: a central absolute
blackness, fading toward deep gray near the edges
where starlight caught an atmosphere more savagely

compressed than Earth's ocean abyss. Through the telescope appeared changeable streaks and mottlings, bands, spots, a hint of color too faint for the eye to tell . . . as if the ghosts of burned-out fires still walked.

Quite oblate, Maclaren reminded himself. *That would have given us a hint, if we'd known. Or the radio spectrum; now I realize, when it's too late, that the lines really* are *triplets, and their broadening is Doppler shift.*

The silence was smothering.

Nakamura drifted in. He poised himself in the air and waited quietly.

"Well?" said Maclaren.

"Sverdlov remains outside, looking at the accelerators and web," said Nakamura. "He will not admit we have no hope."

"Neither will I," said Maclaren.

"Virtually the whole system is destroyed. Fifty meters of it have vanished. The rest is fused, twisted, short-circuited . . . a miracle it continued to give some feeble kind of blast, so I could at least find an orbit." Nakamura laughed. Maclaren thought that that high-pitched, apologetic giggle was going to be hard to live with, if one hadn't been raised among such symbols. "We carry a few spare parts, but not that many."

"Perhaps we can make some," said Maclaren.

"Perhaps," said Nakamura. "But of course the accelerators are of no importance in themselves. The reconstruction of the web is the only way to get home. . . . What has the young man Ryerson to say about that?"

"Don't know. I sent him off to check the manifest and then look over the stuff the ship actually carries. He's been gone a long time, but—"

"I understand," said Nakamura. "It is not easy to face a death sentence when one is young."

Maclaren nodded absently and returned his gaze to the scribbled data sheets he held. After a moment, Nakamura cleared his throat and said awkwardly: "Ah . . . I beg your pardon . . . about the affair of Engineer Sverdlov—"

"Well?" Maclaren didn't glance up from the figures. He had a lot of composure of his own to win back. *The fact is,* he thought through a hammer-beat in his temples, *I am the man afraid. Now that there is nothing I can do, simply a cold waiting until word is given me whether I can live or must die . . . I find that Terangi Maclaren is a coward.*

Sickness was a doubled fist inside his gullet.

"I am not certain what, er, happened," stumbled Nakamura, "and I do not wish to know. If you will be so kind . . . I hope you were not unduly inconvenienced—"

"No. It's all right."

"If we could tacitly ignore it. As I think he has tried to do. The best men have their breaking point."

I always knew that one day would see an end to white sails above green water, and to wine, and Nō masks, and a woman's laughter. I had not expected it yet.

"After all," said Nakamura, "we must work together now."

"Yes." *I had not expected it a light-century from the home of my fathers. My life was spent in having fun, and now I find that the black star has no interest in amusing me.*

"Do you know yet what went wrong?" asked Nakamura. "I would not press you for an answer, but—"

"Oh, yes," said Maclaren. "I know."

Beneath a scrapheap of songs and keels, loves and jokes and victories, which mattered no longer but would not leave him, Maclaren found his brain working with a startling dry clarity. "I'm not sure how much we can admit to the others," he said. "Because this could have been averted, if we'd proceeded with more caution."

"I wondered a little at the time." Nakamura laughed again. "But who would look for danger around a—a corpse?"

"Broadened spectrum lines mean a quickly rotating star," said Maclaren. "Since the ship was not approaching in the equatorial plane, we missed the full Doppler effect, but we might have stopped to think. And tripled lines mean a Zeeman splitting."

"Ah." Nakamura sucked in a hiss of air. "Magnetism?"

"The most powerful bloody magnetic field ever noticed around any heavenly body," said Maclaren. "Judging from the readings I get here, the polar field is . . . oh, I can't say yet. Five, six, seven thousand gauss—somewhere on that order of magnitude. Fantastic! Sol's field is 53 gauss. They don't ever go much above 2,000. Except here."

He rubbed his chin. "Dynamo effect, at that level below the surface where degenerate matter is under such conditions that it's superconductive." The steadiness of his words was a faintly pleasing surprise to him. "Magnetic field becomes directly related to angular velocity. The reason no sun we've known before has a field like this thing here is that it would have to rotate too fast. Couldn't take the strain; it would go whoomp and scatter pieces of star from hell to tiffin." An odd, perverse comfort in speaking lightly: a lie to oneself, persuading the subconscious mind that its companions were not doomed men and a black sun, but an amorous girl waiting for the next jest in a Citadel tavern. "As this star collapsed on itself, after burning out, it had to spin faster, d' you see? Conservation of angular momentum. It seems to have had an unusual amount to start with, of course, but the rotational speed is chiefly a result of its degenerate state. And that same super-density allows it to twirl with such indecent haste. You might say the bursting strength is immensely greater.''

"Yes," said Nakamura. "I see."

"I've been making some estimates," said Maclaren. "It didn't actually take a very strong field to wreck us. We could easily have been protected against it. Any ion-drive craft going close to a planet is—a counter-magnetic circuit with a feedback loop—elementary. But naturally, these big ships were not meant to land anywhere. They would certainly never approach a live sun this close, and the possibility of this black dwarf having such a vicious magnetism—well, no one ever thought of it.''

He shrugged. "Figure it out yourself, Captain Nakamura. The old H, e, v formula. A proton traveling at three-fourths c down a hundred-meter tube is deflected one centimeter by a field of seven one-hundredths gauss. We entered such a field at a million kilometers out, more or less. A tenuous but extremely energetic stream of ionized gas hit the outermost accelerator ring. I make the temperature equivalent of that velocity to be something like three million million degrees Kelvin, if I remember the value of the gas constant correctly. The closer to the star we got, the stronger field we were in, so the farther up the ions struck.

"Of course," finished Maclaren in a tired voice, "these quantities are just estimates, using simple algebra. Since we slanted across the magnetic field, you'd need a vectorial differential equation to describe exactly what happened. You might find occasion to change my figures by a factor of five or six. But I think I have the general idea.''

"Yes-s-s," said Nakamura, "I think you do."

They hung side by side in dimness and looked out at the eye-hurting bright stars.

"Do you know," said Maclaren, "there is one sin

which is punished with unfailing certainty, and must therefore be the deadliest sin in all time. Stupidity.''

"I am not so sure." Nakamura's reply jarred him a little, by its sober literal-mindedness. "I have known many—well, shall I call them unintellectual?—people who lived happy and useful lives.''

"I wasn't referring to that kind of stupidity." Maclaren went through the motions of a chuckle. "I meant our own kind. Yours and mine. We bear the guilt, you know. We should have stopped and thought the situation over before rushing in. I did want to approach more slowly, measuring as we went, and you overruled me.''

"I am ashamed," said Nakamura. He bent his face toward his hands.

"No, let me finish. I should have come here with a well-thought-out program in mind. I gave you no valid reasons *not* to establish a close-in orbit at once. My sole grumble was that you wouldn't allow me time to take observations as we went toward the star. You were perfectly justified, on the basis of the information available to you— Oh, the devils take it! I bring this up only so you'll know what topics to avoid with our shipmates—who must also bear some of the blame for not thinking—because we can't afford quarrels." Maclaren felt his cheeks crease in a sort of grin. "I have no interest in the guilt question anyway. My problem is strictly pragmatic: I want out of here!''

Ryerson emerged from the living-quarter screen. Maclaren saw him first as a shadow. Then the young face came so near that he could see the eyes unnaturally bright and the lips shaking.

"What have you found, Dave?" The question ripped from him before he thought.

Ryerson looked away from them both. Thickly: "We can't do it. We don't carry enough replacement parts to make a f-f-functioning . . . a web—we can't.''

"I knew that," said Nakamura. "Of course. But we have instruments and machine tools. There is bar metal in the hold, which we can shape to our needs. The main problem is—"

"Is where to get four kilos of pure germanium!" Ryerson screamed it. The walls sneered at him with echoes. "Down on that star, maybe?"

9

SQUARE AND INHUMAN in a spacesuit, Sverdlov led
the way through the engine-room airlock. When
Ryerson, following, stepped forth onto the ship's
hull, he entered a moment outside existence.

He snatched for his breath. Alien suns went
streaming past his head. Otherwise he knew
blackness, touched by meaningless dull splashes. He
clawed after anything real. The motion tore him
loose and he went spinning outward toward the dead
star. But he felt it just as a tide of nausea; his ears
roared at him, the scrambled darks and gleams made
a wheel with himself crucified at the hub. He was
never sure if he screamed.

The lifeline jerked him to a halt. He rebounded,
more slowly. Sverdlov's sardonic voice struck his earphones: "Don't be so jumpy next time, Earthling,"

and he gained a sense of direction as the Krasnan began to reel him in.

Suddenly Ryerson made out a pattern. The circle of shadow before him was the hull. The metallic shimmers projecting from it . . . oh, yes, one of the auxiliary tank attachments. The mass-ratio needed to reach one-half c with an exhaust velocity of three-fourths c is $4 \cdot 35$—relativistic formulas apply rather than the simple Newtonian exponential—and this must be squared for deceleration. The *Cross* had left Sol with a tank of mercury on either side, feeding into the fuel deck. Much later, the empty containers had been knocked down into parts of the aircraft now stowed inboard.

Ryerson pulled his mind back from the snugness of engineering data. Beyond the hull, and around it, behind him, for x billion light-years on every side, lay the stars. The nearer ones flashed and glittered and stabbed his eyes, uncountably many; he could not have picked out a single constellation if his training had not included study of simulacra. The outlines they scrawled were unlike those Ryerson remembered from Earth: even the recognizable ones, such as Sagittarius, were distorted, and he felt that as a somehow ghastly thing, as if it were his wife's face which had melted and run. The farther stars blended into the Milky Way, a single clotted swoop around the sky, the coldest color in all reality. And yet farther away, beyond a hundred thousand or a million light-years, he could see more stars—billions at a time, formed into the tiny blue-white blurs of other galaxies.

Impact jarred Ryerson's feet. He stood erect, his bootsoles holding him by a weak stickiness to the plastic hull. Rotation made the sky move slowly past his gaze. It created a dim sense of hanging head down; he thought of ghosts come back to the world like squeaking bats. His eyes sought Sverdlov's vague, armored shape. It was so solid and ugly a form that he could have wept his gratitude.

"All right," grunted the Krasnan. "Let's go."

They moved precariously around the curve of the ship. The long thin frame-sections lashed across their backs vibrated to their cautious footfalls. When they reached the lattice jutting from the stern, Sverdlov halted. "Show you a trick," he said. "Light doesn't diffuse in vacuum, makes it hard to see an object in the round, so—" He squeezed a small plastic bag with one gauntleted hand. His flashbeam snapped on, to glow through a fine mist in front of him. "It's a heavy organic liquid. Forms droplets which hang around for hours before dissipating. Now, what d' you think of the transceiver web?"

Ryerson stooped awkwardly, scrambled about peering for several minutes, and finally answered: "It bears out what you reported. I think this can be repaired. But we'll have to take most of the parts inboard, perhaps melt them down—re-machine them, at least. And we'll need wholly new sections to replace what boiled away. Have we adequate bar metal for that?"

"Guess so. Then what?"

"Then—" Ryerson felt sweat form beneath his armpits and break off in little globs. "You understand I am a tachyonicist, not a mattercasting engineer. A physicist would not be the best possible man to design a bridge; likewise, there's much I'll have to teach myself, to carry this out. But I can use the operating manual, and calculate a lot of quantities afresh, and . . . well . . . I think I could recreate a functioning web. The tuning will be strictly cut-and-try: you have to have exact resonance to get any effect at all, and the handbook assumes that such components as the distortion oscillator will have precise, standardized dimensions and crystal structure. Since they won't—we haven't the facilities to control it, even if I could remember what the quantities are— Well, once we've rebuilt what looks like a workable web, I'll have to try out different combinations of settings, perhaps for weeks, until . . . well, Sol or Centauri or . . . or any of the stations, even another spaceship . . . resonates—"

"Are you related to a Professor Broussard of Lomonosov Academy?" interrupted the other man.

"Why, no. What—"

"You lecture just like he used to. I am not interested in the theory and practice of mattercasting. I want to know, can we get home?"

Ryerson clenched a fist. He was glad that helmets and darkness hid their two faces. "Yes," he said. "If all goes well. And if we can find four kilos of germanium."

"What do you want that for?"

"Do you see those thick junction points in the web? They are, uh, you might call them giant transistors. Half the lattice is gone: there, the germanium was simply whiffed away. I do know the crystallo-chemical structure involved. And we can get the other elements needed by cannibalizing, and an alloying unit aboard could be adapted to manufacture the transistors themselves. But we don't have four spare kilos of germanium."

Sverdlov's tone grew heavy with skepticism: "And that balloonhead Maclaren means to find a planet? And mine the stuff?"

"I don't know—" Ryerson wet his lips. "I don't know what else we can do."

"But this star went supernova!"

"It was a big star. It would have had many planets. Some of the outermost ones—if they were large to start with—may have survived."

"Ha! And you'd hunt around on a lump of fused nickel-iron, without even a sun in the sky, for germanium ore?"

"We have an isotope separator. It could be adapted to— I haven't figured it out yet, but— For God's sake!" Ryerson found himself screaming. "What else can we do?"

"Shut up!" rasped Sverdlov. "When I want my earphones broken I'll use a hammer."

He stood in a swirl of golden fog, and the gray-rimmed black eye of the dead star marched behind him. Ryerson crouched back, hooked into the framework and waiting. At last Sverdlov said: "It's one long string of ifs. But a transistor doesn't do anything a vacuum tube can't." He barked a laugh. "And we've got all the vacuum we'll ever want. Why not design and make the equivalent electronic elements? Ought to be a lot easier than—repairing the accelerators, and scouring space for a planet."

"Design them?" cried Ryerson. "And test them, and redesign them, and— Do you realize that on half rations we have not quite six months' food supply?"

"I do," said Sverdlov. "I feel it in my belly right now." He muttered a few obscenities. "All right, then. I'll go along with the plan. Though if that clot-brain of a Nakamura hadn't—"

"He did the only thing possible! Did you *want* to crash us?"

"There are worse chances to take," said Sverdlov. "Now what have we got, but six months of beating our hearts out and then another month or two to die?" He made a harsh noise in the radiophone, as if wanting to spit. "I've met Sarai settlers before. They're worse than Earthlings for cowardice, and nearly as stupid."

"Now, wait—" began Ryerson. "Wait, let's not quarrel—"

"Afraid of what might happen?" jeered Sverdlov. "You don't know your friend Maclaren's dirty-fighting tricks, do you?"

The ship whirled through a darkness that grew

noisy with Ryerson's uneven breathing. He raised his
hands against the bulky robot shape confronting
him. "Please," he stammered. "Now wait, wait,
Engineer Sverdlov." Tears stung his eyes. "We're all
in this together, you know."

"I wondered when you'd be coming up with that
cliché," snorted the Krasnan. "Having decided it
would be oh, so amusing to tell your society friends,
how you spent maybe a whole month in deep space,
you got me yanked off the job I really want to do,
and tossed me into a situation you'd never once
stopped to think about, and wrecked us—and now
you tell me, 'We're all in this together'!" Suddenly
he roared his words: "You mangy son of a muck-
eating cockroach, I'll get you back—not for your
sake, nor for your wife's, because if she's an
Earthling I know how she'll be spending the time
you're gone—but for my own planet, d' you hear?
They need me there!"

It grew very still. Ryerson felt how his heartbeat
dropped down to normal, and then further, until he
could no longer hear his own pulse. His hands felt
chilly and his face numb. A far and terrified part of
him thought, *So this is how it feels, when the God of
Hosts lays His hand upon a man,* but he stared past
Sverdlov, into the relentless white blaze of the stars,
and said in a flat voice:

"That will do. I've heard the story of the poor op-
pressed colonies before now. I think you yourself are
proof that the Protectorate is better than you deserve. As for me, I never saw a milli of this supposed
extortion from other planets: my father worked his
way up from midshipman to captain, my brothers
and I went through the Academy on merit, as citizens
of the poorest and most overcrowded world in the
universe. Do you imagine you know what com-
petition is? Why, you blowhard clodhopper, you
wouldn't last a week on Earth. As a matter of fact, I

myself had grown tired of the struggle. If it weren't for this wretched expedition, my wife and I would have started for a new colony next week. Now you make me wonder if it's wise. Are all colonials like you—barely brave enough to slander an old man and a woman when they're a safe hundred light-years away?''

Sverdlov did not move. The slow spin of the *Cross* brought the black star into Ryerson's view again. It seemed bigger, as the ship swooped toward periastron. He had a horrible sense of falling into it. *Thou, God, watchest me, with the ashen eye of wrath.* The silence was like a membrane stretched close to ripping.

Finally the bass voice came. "Are you prepared to back up those words, Earthling?''

"Right after we finish here!" shouted Ryerson.

"Oh." A moment longer. Then: "Forget it. Maybe I did speak out of turn. I've never known an Earthman who wasn't . . . an enemy of some kind.''

"Did you ever try to know them?''

"Forget it, I said. I'll get you home. I might even come around one day and say hello, on your new planet. But let's get busy here. Our first job is to start the accelerators operating again.''

The weakness which poured through David Ryerson was such that he wondered if he would have fallen under gravity. *Oh, Tamara,* he thought, *be with me now.* He remembered how they had camped on a California beach . . . had it quite to themselves, no one lived in the deserts eastward . . . and the gulls had swarmed around begging bread until both of them were helpless with laughter. Now why should he suddenly remember that, out of all the times they had had?

10

WHEN THE MIND gave up and the mathematics became a blur, work awaited Maclaren's hands. Sverdlov, and Ryerson under him, did the machine-tool jobs; Nakamura's small fingers showed such delicacy that he was set to drawing wire and polishing control-ring surfaces. Maclaren was left with the least skilled assignment, least urgent because he was always far ahead of the consumption of his product: melting, separating, and re-alloying the fused salvage from ion accelerators and transceiver web.

But it was tricky in null-gee. They could not have any significant spin on the ship or assembly, out on the lattice, would have become too complicated for so small a gang of workers. Coriolis force would have created serious problems for the inboard jobs too. On the other hand, weightless melt had foul habits. Maclaren's left arm was still bandaged, the burn on his forehead still a crimson gouge.

It didn't seem to matter. When he looked in a mirror, he hardly recognized his face. There hadn't been much physical change yet, but the expression was a stranger's. And his life had narrowed to these past weeks; behind them lay only a dream. In moments when he had nothing else to do he might play a quick chess game with Sverdlov, argue the merits of Nō versus Kabuki with Nakamura, or shock young Ryerson with a well-chosen dirty limerick. But thinking back, he saw how such times had become more and more sparse. He had quit trying to make iron rations palatable, when his turn in the galley came up; he had not sung a ballad for hundreds of the *Cross'* black-sun years. He shaved by the clock and hung on to fastidiousness of dress as pure ritual, the way Nakamura contemplated his paradoxes or Ryerson quoted his Bible or Sverdlov thumbed through his nude photographs of past mistresses. It was a way of telling yourself, *I remain alive.*

A moment came when Maclaren asked himself what he was doing other than go through the motions of survival. That was a bad question.

"You see," he told his mirror twin, "it suggests a further inquiry: Why? And that's the problem we've been dodging all our mutual days."

He stowed his electric razor, adjusted his tunic, and pushed out of the tiny bathroom. The living section was deserted, as it had been most of the time. Not only was everyone too busy to sit around, but it was too narrow.

Outside its wall, he moved through the comfort of his instruments. He admitted frankly that his project of learning as much as possible of the star was three-quarters selfish. It was not really very probable that exact knowledge of its atmospheric composition would be of any use to their escape. But it offered him a chance, for minutes at a time, to forget where he was. Of course, he did not admit the fact to anyone but himself. And he wondered a little what reticences his shipmates had.

This time he was not alone. Nakamura hovered at an observation port. The pilot's body was outlined with unwavering diamond stars. But as the dead sun swung by, Maclaren saw him grow tense and bring a hand toward his eyes, as if to cover them.

He drifted soundlessly behind Nakamura. "Boo," he said.

The other whirled around in air, gasping. As the thresh of arms and legs died away, Maclaren looked upon terror.

"I'm sorry!" he exclaimed. "I didn't think I'd startle you."

"I . . . it is nothing." Nakamura's brown gaze held some obscure beggary. "I should not have— It is nothing."

"Did you want anything of me?" Maclaren offered one of his last cigarets. Nakamura accepted it blindly, without saying thanks. *Something is terribly wrong with this lad,* thought Maclaren. Fear drained in through the glittering viewport. *And he's the only pilot we've got.*

"No. I had—I was resting a few moments. One cannot do precision work when . . . tired . . . yes-s-s." Nakamura's hunger-gaunted cheeks caved in with the violence of his sucking on the tobacco. A little crown of sweat-beads danced around his head.

"Oh, you're not bothering me." Maclaren crossed his legs and leaned back on the air. "As a matter of fact, I'm glad of your company. I need someone to talk with."

Nakamura laughed his meaningless laugh. "We should look to you for help, rather than you to us," he said. "You are the least changed of us all."

"Oh? I thought I was the most affected. Sverdlov hankers for his women and his alcohol and his politics. Ryerson wants back to his shiny new wife and his shiny new planet. You're the local rock of ages. But me—" Maclaren shrugged. "I've nothing to anchor me."

"You have grown quieter, yes." The cigaret in Nakamura's hand quivered a trifle, but his words came steadily now.

"I have begun to wonder about things." Maclaren scowled at the black sun. By treating it as a scientific problem, he had held at arm's length the obsession he had seen eating at Ryerson—who grew silent and large-eyed and reverted to the iron religion he had once been shaking off—and at Sverdlov, who waxed bitterly profane. So far, Maclaren had not begun thinking of the star as a half-alive malignancy. But it would be far too easy to start.

"One does, sooner or later." Nakamura's tone held no great interest. He was still wrapped up in his private horror, and that was what Maclaren wanted to get him out of.

"But I don't wonder efficiently. I find myself going blank, when all I'm really doing is routine stuff and I could just as well be thinking at my problems."

"Thought is a technique, to be learned," said Nakamura, "just as the uses of the body—" He broke off. "I have no right to teach. I have failed my own masters."

"I'd say you were doing very well. I've envied you your faith. You have an answer."

"Zen does not offer any cut-and-dried answers to problems. In fact, it tries to avoid theory. No human system can comprehend the infinite real universe."

"I know."

"And that is my failure," whispered Nakamura. "I look for an explanation. I do not want merely to be. No, that is not enough . . . out here, I find that I want to be justified."

Maclaren stared into the cruelty of heaven. "I'll tell you something," he said. "I'm scared spitless."

"What? But I thought—"

"Oh, I have plenty of flip retorts to camouflage it. But I'm as much afraid to die, I'm struggling as frantically and with as little dignity, as any trapped rat. And I'm slowly coming to see why, too. It's because I haven't got anything but my own life—my own minute meaningless life of much learning and no understanding, much doing and no accomplishing, many acquaintances and no friends—it shouldn't be worth the trouble of salvaging, should it? And yet I'm unable to see any more in the entire universe than that: a lot of scurrying small accidents of organic chemistry, on a lot of flyspeck planets. If things made even a little sense, if I could see anything more important than this bunch of mucous membranes labeled Terangi Maclaren . . . why, then there'd be no reason to fear my own termination. The things that mattered would go on."

Nakamura smoked in silence for a while. Maclaren finished his own cigaret in quick nervous puffs, fought temptation, swore to himself and lit another.

"I didn't mean to turn you into a weeping post," he said. And he thought: *The hell I didn't. I fed you your psychological medicine right on schedule. Though perhaps I did make the dose larger than planned.*

"I am unworthy," said Nakamura. "But it is an honor." He stared outward, side by side with the other man. "I try to reassure myself with the thought that there must be beings more highly developed than we," he said.

"Are you sure?" answered Maclaren, welcoming the chance to be impersonal. "We've never found any that were even comparable to us. In the brains department, at least. I'll admit the Van Maanen's abos are more beautiful, and the Old Thothians more reliable and sweet-tempered."

"How much do we know of the galaxy?"

"Um-m-m . . . yes."

"I have lived in the hope of encountering a truly great race. If they are not like gods—they will at least have their own wise men. They will not look at the world as we do. From each other, two such peoples could learn the unimaginable, just as the high epochs of Earth's history came when different peoples interflowed. Yes-s-s. But this would be so much more, because the difference is greater. Less conflict. What reason for it? More to offer, a billion years of separate experience as life-forms."

"I can tell you this much," said Maclaren, "the Protectorate would not like it. Our present civilization couldn't survive such a transfusion of ideas."

"Is our civilization anything so great?" asked Nakamura with an unwonted scornfulness.

"No. I suppose not."

"We have a number of technical tricks. Doubtless we could learn more from such aliens as I am thinking of. But what we would really learn that mattered—for this era of human history lacks one—would be a philosophy."

"I thought you didn't believe in philosophies."

"I used a wrong word. I meant a *dō*—a way. A way of . . . an attitude? That is what life is for, that is your 'Why'—it is not a mechanical cause-and-effect thing, it is the spirit in which we live."

Nakamura laughed again. "But hear the child correcting the master! I, who cannot follow the known precepts of Zen, ask for help from the unknown! Were it offered me, I would doubtless crawl into the nearest worm-hole.''

And suddenly the horror flared up again. He grabbed Maclaren's arm. It sent them both twisting around, so that their outraged senses of balance made the stars whirl in their skulls. Maclaren felt Nakamura's grip like ice on his bare skin.

"I am afraid!" choked the pilot. "Help me! I am afraid!"

They regained their floating positions. Nakamura let go and took a fresh cigaret with shaking fingers. The silence grew thick.

Maclaren said at last, not looking toward the Saraian: "Why not tell me the reason? It might relieve you a bit."

Nakamura drew a breath. "I have always been afraid of space," he said. "And yet called to it also. Can you understand?"

"Yes. I think I know."

"It has—" Nakamura giggled—"unsettled me. All my life. First, as a child I was taken from my home on Earth, across space. And now, of course, I can never come back."

"I have some pull in the Citadel. A visa could be arranged."

"You are too kind. I am not sure whether it would help. Kyoto cannot be as I remember it. If it has not changed, surely I have, yes-s-s? But please let me continue. After a few years on Sarai, my whole family, except my brother and me, were killed by a meteor fall that struck our home. Stones from space, do you see? We did not think of it that way, then. The monastery raised us. We made a voyage together as cadets. Have you heard of the *Firdausi* disaster?"

"No, I'm afraid not." Maclaren poured smoke from his mouth, as a veil against the cosmos.

"Forty Eridani is actually a triple star. The *Firdausi* had been long at the airless innermost planet of one of the red dwarfs, a remote-controlled survey trip. It shines feebly, that sun . . . but it flared, as its kind of star is apt to do, a giant flare. Those radiations caused a metal fatigue. No one suspected. On our cruise, later, with men aboard, the ship suddenly failed. The pilot barely got us into an orbit, after we had fallen a long way toward our own sun. There we had to wait until rescue came. Many died from the heat. My brother was one of them."

Stillness hummed.

"I see," said Maclaren at last.

"Since then I have been afraid of space. It rises into my consciousness from time to time." Maclaren stole a glance at Nakamura. The little man was lotus-postured in midair, save that he stared at his hands and they twisted together. Wretchedness overrode his voice. "And yet I could not stop my work either. Because out in space I often seem to come closer to . . . oneness . . . that which we all seek, what you have called understanding. But here, caught in this orbit about this star, the oneness is gone and the fear has grown and grown until I am afraid I will have to scream."

"It might help," said Maclaren.

Nakamura looked up. He tried to smile. "What do you think?" he asked.

Maclaren blew a meditative cloud of smoke. Now he would have to pick his words with care—and no background or training in the giving of succor—or lose the sole man who could pull this ship free. Or lose Nakamura: that aspect of it seemed, all at once, more important.

"I wonder," he murmured, "even in an absolutely free society, if any such thing could exist— I wonder if every man isn't afraid of his bride."

"What?" Nakamura's lids snapped apart in startlement.

"And needs her at the same time," said Maclaren. "I might extend it beyond sex. Perhaps fear is a necessary part of anything that matters. Could Bach have loved his God so magnificently without being inwardly afraid of Him? I don't know."

He stubbed out his cigaret. "I suggest you meditate upon this," he said lightly. "And on the further fact, which may be a little too obvious for you to have seen, that this is not 40 Eridani."

Then he waited.

Nakamura made a gesture with his body. Only afterward, thinking about it, did Maclaren realize it was a free-fall prostration. "Thank you," he said.

"I should thank you," said Maclaren, quite honestly. "You gave me a leg up too, y' know."

Nakamura departed for the machine shop.

Maclaren hung at the viewport a while longer. The rasp of a pocket lighter brought his head around.

Chang Sverdlov entered from the living section. The cigar in his mouth was held at a somehow resentful angle.

"Well," said Maclaren, "how long were you listening?"

"Long enough," grunted the engineer.

He blew cheap, atrocious smoke until his pocked face was lost in it. "So," he asked, "aren't you going to get mad at me?"

"If it serves a purpose," said Maclaren.

"Uh!" Sverdlov fumed away for a minute longer. "Maybe I had that coming," he said.

"Quite probably. But how are the repairs progressing outside?"

"All right. Look here," Sverdlov blurted, "do me a favor, will you? If you can. Don't admit to Ryerson, or me, that you're human—that you're just as scared and confused as the rest of us. Don't admit it to Nakamura, even. You didn't, you know, so far—not really. We need a—a—a damned cocky dude of a born-and-bred technic—to get us through!''

He whirled back into the quarters. Maclaren heard him dive, almost fleeing, aft along the shaftway.

11

NAKAMURA NOTED in the log, which he had religiously maintained, the precise moment when the *Cross* blasted from the dead star. The others had not tried to keep track of days. There were none out here. There was not even time, in any meaningful sense of the word—only existence, with an unreal impression of sunlight and leaves and women before existence began, like an inverted prenatal memory.

The initial minutes of blast were no more veritable. They took their posts and stared without any sense of victory at their instruments. Nakamura in the control turret, Maclaren on the observation deck feeding him data, Sverdlov and Ryerson watchful in the engine room, felt themselves merely doing another task in an infinite succession.

Sverdlov was the first who broke from his cold

womb and knew himself alive. After an hour of poring over his dials and viewscreens, through eyes bulged by two gravities, he ran a hand across the bristles on his jaw. "Holy fecal matter," he whispered. "The canine-descended thing is hanging together."

And perhaps none but Ryerson, who had worked outside with him for weeks of hours, could understand.

The lattice jutting from the sphere had a crude, unfinished look. And indeed little had been done toward restoring the transceiver web; time enough for that while they hunted a planet. Sverdlov had simply installed a framework to support his refashioned accelerator rings, antimagnetic shielding circuits, and incidental wires, tubes, grids, capacitors, transformers. . . . He had tested with a milliampere of ion current, cursed, readjusted, tested again, nodded, asked for a full amp, made obscene comments, readjusted, retested, and wondered if he could have done it without Ryerson. It was not so much that he needed the extra hands, but the boy had been impossibly patient. When Sverdlov could take no more electronic misbehavior, and went back into the ship and got a sledge and pounded at an iron bar for lack of human skulls to break, Ryerson had stayed outside trying a fresh hookup.

Once, when they were alone among galaxies, Sverdlov asked him about it. "Aren't you human, kid? Don't you ever want to throw a rheostat across the room?"

Ryerson's tone came gnat-like in his earphones, almost lost in an endless crackling of cosmic noise. "It doesn't do any good. My father taught me that much. We sailed a lot at home."

"So?"

"The sea never forgives you."

Sverdlov glanced at the other, couldn't find him in

the tricky patching of highlight and blackness, and suddenly confronted Polaris. It was like being stabbed. How many men, he thought with a gasp, had followed the icy North Star to their weird?

"Of course," Ryerson admitted humbly, "it's not so easy to get along with people."

And the lattice grew. And finally it tested sound, and Sverdlov told Nakamura they could depart.

The engine which had accelerated the *Cross* to half light speed could not lift her straight away from this sun. Nor could her men have endured a couple of hundred gravities for however short a time. She moved out at two gees, her gyros holding the blast toward the mass she was escaping, so that her elliptical orbit became a spiral. It would take hours to reach a point where the gravitational field had dropped so far that a hyperbolic path would be practicable.

Sverdlov crouched in his harness, glaring at screens and indicators. The bloody damned dead cinder wasn't going to let them escape this easily! He had stared too long at its ashen face to imagine that. It would play some new trick, and he would have to be ready. God, he was thirsty! The ship did have a water-regenerating unit, merely because astronautical regulations at the time she was built insisted on it. Odd, owing your life to some bureaucrat two hundred years dust on his own filing cabinets. But the regenerator was inadequate and hadn't been used in all that time. No need for it: waste material went into the matter bank, and was reborn as water or food or anything else, according to a signal sent from the Lunar station with every change of watch.

But no more signals were coming to the *Cross*. Food, once eaten, was gone for good. Recycled water was little more than sufficient to maintain life. *Fire and thunder!* thought Sverdlov. *I can smell myself two kilometers away. I might not sell out the*

Fellowship for a bottle of beer, but the Protector had better not offer me a case.

A soft *brroom-brroom-brroom* pervaded his awareness, the engine talked to itself. Too loud, somehow. The instruments read okay, but Sverdlov did not think an engine with a good destiny would make so much noise. He glanced back at the viewscreens. The black sun was scarcely visible. It couldn't be seen at all unless you knew just where to look. The haywired ugliness of the ion drive made a cage for stars. The faintest blue glow wavered down the rings. Shouldn't, of course. Inefficiency. St. Elmo's fire danced near the after end of the assembly. "Engine room to pilot. How are we making out?"

"Satisfactory." Nakamura's voice sounded thin. It must be a strain, yes, he was doing a hundred things manually for which the ship lacked robots. But who could have anticipated—?

Sverdlov narrowed his eyes. "Take a look at the tail of this rig, Dave," he said. "The rear negatron ring. See anything?"

"Well . . ." The boy's eyes, dark-rimmed and bloodshot, went heavily after Sverdlov's pointing finger. "Electrostatic discharge, that blue light—"

"See anything else?" Sverdlov glanced uneasily at the megammeters. He did not have a steady current going down the accelerators, it fluctuated continually by several percent. But was the needle for the negatron side creeping ever so slowly downward?

"No. No, I can't."

"Should'a put a thermocouple in every ring. Might be a very weak deflection of ions, chewing at the endmost till all at once its focusing goes blooey and we're in trouble."

"But we tested every single— And the star's magnetic field is attenuating with every centimeter we advance."

"Vibration, my cub-shaped friend. It'd be easy to shake one of these jury-rigged magnetic coils enough out of alignment to— *Hold it!*"

The terminal starboard coil glowed red. Blue electric fire squirted forth and ran up the lattice. The negative megammeter dropped ten points and Sverdlov felt a little surge as the ship wallowed to one side from an unbalanced thrust.

"Engine room stopping blast!" he roared. His hand had already gone crashing onto the main lever.

The noise whined away to a mumble. He felt himself pitched off a cliff as high as eternity.

"What's the trouble?" barked Maclaren's voice.

Sverdlov relieved himself of a few unrepeatable remarks. "Something's gone sour out there. The last negatron accelerator began to heat and the current to drop. Didn't you feel us yaw?"

"Oh, Lord, have mercy," groaned Ryerson. He looked physically sick. "Not again."

"Ah, it needn't be so bad," said Sverdlov. "Me, I'm surprised the mucking thing held together this long. You can't do much with baling wire and spit, you know." Inwardly, he struggled with a wish to beat somebody's face.

"I presume we are in a stable orbit," said Nakamura. "But I would feel a good deal easier if the repair can·be made soon. Do you want any help?"

"No. Dave and I can handle it. Stand by to give us a test blast."

Sverdlov and Ryerson got into their spacesuits. "I swear this smells fouler every day," said the Krasnan. "I didn't believe I could be such a filth generator." He slapped down his helmet and added into the radio: "So much for man the glorious star-conqueror."

"No," said Ryerson.

"What?"

"The stinks are only the body. That isn't important. What counts is the soul inside."

Sverdlov cocked his bullet head and stared at the other armored shape. "Do you actually believe that guff?"

"I'm sorry, I didn't mean to preach or—"

"Never mind. I don't feel like arguing either." Sverdlov laughed roughly. "I'll give you one thing to mull over, though. If the body's such a valueless piece of pork, and we'll all meet each other in the sweet bye and bye, and so on, why're you busting every gut you own to get back to your wife?"

He heard an outraged breath in his earphones. For a moment he felt he had failed somehow. There was no room here for quarrels. *Ah, shaft it,* he told himself. *If an Earthling don't like to listen to a colonial, he can jingle-bang well stay out of space.*

They gathered tools and instruments in a silence that smoldered. When they left the airlock, they had the usual trouble in seeing. Then their pupils expanded and their minds switched over to the alien gestalt. A raw blaze leaped forth and struck them.

Feeling his way aft along the lattice, Sverdlov sensed his anger bleed away. The boy was right—it did no good to curse dead matter. Save your rage for those who needed it, tyrants and knaves and their sycophants. And you might even wonder (it was horrible to think) if they were worth it either. He stood with ten thousand bitter suns around him; but none were Sol or Tau Ceti. O Polaris, death's lodestar, are we as little as all that?

He reached the end of the framework, clipped his lifeline on, and squirted a light-diffusing fog at the ring. Not too close, he didn't want it to interfere with his ion stream, but it gave him three-dimensional illumination. He let his body float out behind while he pulled himself squinting-close to the accelerator.

"Hm, yes, it's been pitted," he said. "Naturally it

would be the negatron side which went wrong.
Protons do a lot less harm, striking normal matter.
Hand me that counter, will you?''

Ryerson, wordless and faceless, gave him the instrument. Sverdlov checked for radioactivity. ''Not
enough to hurt,'' he decided. ''We won't have to
replace this ring, we stopped the process in time. By
readjusting the magnetic coils we can compensate for
the change in the electric focusing field caused by its
gnawed-up shape. I hope.''

Ryerson said nothing. *Good grief,* thought Sverdlov, *did I offend him that much?* Hitherto they had
talked a bit when working outside, not real conversation but a trivial remark now and then, a grunt for
response . . . just sufficient to drown out the hissing
of the stars.

''Hello, pilot. Give me a microamp. One-second
duration.''

Sverdlov moved out of the way. Even a millionth
of an ampere blast should be avoided, if it was an an-
tiproton current.

Electric sparks crawled like ivy over the bones of
the accelerator. Sverdlov, studying the instruments
he had planted along the ion path, nodded. ''What's
the potentiometer say, Dave?'' he asked. ''If it's
saying anything fit to print, I mean.''

''Standard,'' snapped Ryerson.

Maybe I should apologize, thought Sverdlov. And
then, in a geyser: *Judas, no! If he's that thin-
skinned, he can rot before I do.*

The stars swarmed barely out of reach. Sometimes
changes in the eyeball made them seem to move. Like
flies. A million burning flies. Sverdlov swatted, un-
thinkingly, and snarled to himself.

After a while it occurred to him that Ryerson's
nerves must also be rubbed pretty thin. You
shouldn't expect the kid to act absolutely sensibly. *I
lost my own head at the very start of this affair,*

thought Sverdlov. The memory thickened his temples with blood. He began unbolting the Number One magnetic coil as if it were an enemy to emasculate.

"Okay, gimme another microamp one-second test."

"Try shifting Number Two a few centimeters forward," said Ryerson.

"You crazy?" snorted Sverdlov. *Yes, I suppose we're all a bit crazy by now.* "Look, if the deflected stream strikes here, you'll want to bend it down like so and—"

"Never mind." Ryerson could not be seen to move, in the bulk of his armor, but Sverdlov imagined him turning away with a contemptuous shrug. It took several minutes of tinkering for the Krasnan to realize that the Earthling had visualized the interplay of forces correctly.

He swallowed. "You were right," he emitted.

"Well, let's get it reassembled," said Ryerson coldly.

Very good, Earth snob, sir. Sverdlov attacked the coils for several more minutes. "Test blast." Not quite. Try another setting. "Test blast. Repeat." That seemed to be it. "Give me a milliamp this time. . . . A full amp . . . hm-m." The current had flowed too short a time to heat the ring, but needles wavered wildly.

"We're still getting some deflection," said Sverdlov. "Matter of velocity distribution. A certain small percentage of the particles have abnormal velocities and—" He realized he was crouched under Ryerson's hidden eyes babbling the obvious. "I'll try sliding this one a wee bit more aside. Gimme that vernier wrench. . . . So. One amp test blast, please."

There was no further response from the instruments. Ryerson let out a whistling sigh. "We seem to have done it," he said.

We? thought Sverdlov. *Well, you handed me a few tools!*

Aloud: "We won't know for sure till full thrust is applied."

"Of course." Ryerson spoke hesitantly. Sverdlov recognized the tone; it was trying to be warm. Ryerson was over his fit of temper.

Well, I'm not!

"Nothing to be done about that except to try it and see, is there?" went on the Earthling.

"And if we still get significant deflection, drag on our suits and crawl back here—maybe a dozen times? No!"

"Why, that was how we did it before."

"I'm getting awfully hungry," said Sverdlov. Suddenly it flared out of him. "I'm sick of it! I'm sick of being cooped up in my own stink, and yours, I'm sick of the same stupid faces and the same stupid remarks, yes, the same stars! I've had my fill! Get on back inside. I'll stay here and watch under acceleration. If anything goes wrong, I'll be right on the spot to fix it."

"But—"

Nakamura's voice crackled above the mutter of the galaxy. "What are you thinking of, Engineer Sverdlov? Two gravities would pull you off the ship! And we're not maneuverable enough to rescue you."

"This lifeline is tested for two thousand kilos," said the Krasnan. "It's standard procedure to make direct high-acceleration checks on the blast."

"By automatic instruments."

"Which we haven't got. Do you *know* the system is fully adjusted? Are you so sure there isn't some small cumulative effect, so the thing will quit on you one day when you need it the most?"

Maclaren's tone joined in, dry and somehow remote: "This is a curious time to think about that."

"I am the engineer," said Sverdlov stiffly. "Read

the ship's articles again."

"Well," said Nakamura. "Well, but—"

"It would save time," said Ryerson. "Maybe several days' worth of time, if the coils really are badly maladjusted."

"Thanks, Dave," said Sverdlov clumsily.

"Well," said Nakamura, "you have the authority, of course. But I ask you again—"

"All I ask of *you* is two gravities' worth of oof for a few seconds," interrupted Sverdlov. "When I'm satisfied this ring will function properly, so we won't have to be forever making stops like this, I'll come inside."

He hooked his legs about the framework and began resetting the instruments clamped onto it. "Get on back, Dave," he said.

"Why . . . I thought I would—"

"No need to."

"But there is! You can't read every dial simultaneously, and if there's work to be done you'll need help."

"I'll call you if I want you. Give me your tool belt." Sverdlov took it from reluctant hands and buckled it around himself. "We have got a certain amount of hazard involved, Dave. If I should be unlucky, you're the closest approximation to an engineer the ship will have. She can't spare both of us."

"But why take any risk at all?"

"Because I'm sick of being here! Because I've got to fight back at that damned black coal or start howling! Now get inside!"

As he watched the other blocky shape depart him, Sverdlov thought: *I am actually not being too rational, am I now? But who could expect it, a hundred light-years from the sun?*

As he made ready, he puzzled over what had driven him. He felt a need to wrestle something tangible; and surely to balance on this skeleton of metal, under twice his normal weight, was a challenge. Beyond that, less important really, was the logic of it: the reasons he had given were sound as far as they went, and you could starve to death while proceeding at the pace of caution.

And below everything, he thought, was a dark wish he did not understand. Li-Tsung of Krasna would have told him to live at all costs, sacrifice all the others, to save himself for his planet and the Fellowship. But there were limits. You didn't have to accept Dave's Calvinism—though its unmerciful God seemed very near this dead star—to swallow the truth that some things were more important than survival. Than even the survival of a cause.

Maybe I'm trying to find out what those things are, he thought confusedly.

He crawled "up" till his feet were braced on a cross-member, with the terminal accelerator ring by his right ankle but the electroprober dial conveniently near his faceplate. His right hand gripped a vernier wrench, his left drew taut the lifeline. "Stand by for blast," he said into his radio. "Build up to two gees over a one-minute period, then hold it till I say cut."

Nothing happened for a while except the crawling of the constellations as gyros brought the ship around. Good boy, Seiichi! He'd get some escape distance out of a test blast too. "Stand by," it said in Sverdlov's earphones. And his weight came back to him, until he felt an exultant straining in the muscles of shoulder and arm and leg and belly; until his heart thudded loud enough to drown out the thin crackling talk of the stars.

The hull was above him now, a giant sphere upheld on twin derricks. Down the middle of each derrick guttered a ghostly blue light, and sparks writhed and fountained at junction points. The constellations shone chill through the electric discharge.

Inefficient, thought Sverdlov. *The result of reconstruction without adequate instruments. But it's pretty. Like festival fireworks.* He remembered a pyrotechnic display once, when he was small. His mother had taken him. They sat on a hired catamaran and watched wonder explode softly above the lake.

"Uh," grunted Sverdlov. He narrowed his eyes to peer at the detector dial. There certainly was a significant deflection yet, when whole grams of matter were being thrown out every second. It didn't heat up the ring much, perhaps too little to notice; but negatrons plowed through electron shells, into positive nuclei, and atoms were destroyed. Presently would come crystal deformation, fatigue, ultimate failure. He reported his findings and added with a sense of earned boasting: "I was right. This had to be done."

"I shall halt blast, then. Stand by."

Weightlessness came back. Sverdlov reached out delicately with his wrench, nipped a coil nut, and loosened the bolt. He shifted the coil itself backward. "I'll have this fixed in a minute. There! Now give me three gees for thirty seconds, to make sure."

"Three? Are you certain you—"

"I am. Fire!"

It came to Sverdlov that this was another way a man might serve his planet: simply by being the right kind of man. Maybe a better way than planning the extinction of people who happened to live somewhere else. *Oh, come off it,* he told himself. *Next thing you'll be teaching a Humane League kindergarten.*

The force on him climbed, and his muscles rejoiced in it.

At three gees, he found no deflection against the ring . . . or did he? He peered closer. His right hand, weighted by the tool it still bore, slipped from the member on which it had been leaning. Sverdlov was thrown off balance. He flung both arms wide, instinctively trying not to fall. His right went between the field coils and into the negatron stream.

Fire spouted.

Nakamura cut the drive. Sverdlov hung free, staring by starlight at his arm. The blast had sliced it across as cleanly as an industrial torch. Blood and water vapor rushed out and froze in a little cloud, pale among the nebulae.

There was no pain. Not yet. But his eardrums popped as pressure fell. "Engine room!" he snapped. A part of him stood aside and marveled at his own mind. What a survival machine, when the need came! "Emergency! Drop total accelerator voltage to one thousand. Give me about ten amps down the tube. Quick!"

He felt no weight; such a blast didn't exert enough push on the hull to move it appreciably. He thrust his arm back into the ion stream. Pain did come now, but in his head, as the eardrums ruptured. One minute more and he would have the bends. The gas of antiprotons roared without noise around the stump of his wrist. Steel melted. Sverdlov prodded with a hacksaw gripped in his left hand, trying to seal the spacesuit arm shut.

He seemed far away from everything. Night ate at his brain. He asked himself once in wonderment: "Was I planning to do this to other men?"

When he thought the sleeve was sealed, he withdrew it. "Cut blast," he whispered. "Come and get me." His airtanks fed him oxygen, pressure climbed again inside the suit. It was good to float at the end of a lifeline, breathing. Until he began to strangle on his own blood. Then he gave up and accepted the gift of darkness.

12

NOW, ABOUT WINTER SOLSTICE, day was a pale glimmer, low in the south among steel-colored clouds. Tamara had been walking since the first light sneaked across the ocean, and already the sun was close to setting. She wondered if space itself could be blacker than this land. At least you saw the stars in space. On Skula you huddled indoors against the wind, and the sky was a blind whirl of snow.

A few dry flakes gusted as she came down off the moor to the beach. But they carried no warmth with them, there was not going to be a snowfall tonight. The wind streaked in from a thousand kilometers of Atlantic and icebergs. She felt the cold snap its teeth together around her; a hooded cloak was scant protection. But she *would* not go back to the house. Not till day had drained from the world and it would be unsafe to remain outdoors.

She said to herself, drearily: *I would stay here even then, except it might harm the child, and the old man would come looking for me. David, help me, I don't know which would be worse!*

She knew a twisted pleasure in being so honest with herself. By all the conventions, she should be thinking only of David's unborn baby, herself no more than its vessel. But it was not real to her . . . not yet . . . so far it was sickness in the mornings and bad dreams at night. The reality was Magnus Ryerson, animal-like hairiness and a hoarse grumble at her for not doing the housework his way and incomprehensible readings aloud—his island and his sea and his bloody damned language lessons!

Tamara found herself voicing the curses. "Bloody damned English! Bloody damned English! You can take your language and you know what you can do with it!" She had heard the expression now and then—overheard it, rather, as a small girl peeping through doors while men talked—some of the coarser sort used such phrases, fish ranchers or coral miners or cattle guards. She was not sure what it was everybody knew could be done with it. Tear it into bits, probably, and fling it on the wind, into the ugly Northern ocean.

For a moment her hands clawed together. If she could so destroy Magnus Ryerson!

She fought for decorum. She was a lady. Not a technic, but still a professor's daughter; she could read and write, she had learned to dance and play the flute, pour tea and embroider a dress and converse with learned men so they were not too bored while waiting for her father . . . the arts of graciousness. Her father would call it contrasocial, to hate her husband's father. This was her family now.

But.

Her boots picked a way down the hillside, through snow and heather bushes, until she emerged on a beach of stones. The sea came directly in here, smashing at heaped boulders with a violence that shivered through the ground. She saw how the combers exploded where they struck. Spindrift stung her skin. Beyond the rocks reached a gray waste of galloping white-bearded waves, and the wind keening down from the Pole. It rolled and boomed and whistled out there.

She remembered a living greenish blue of southern waters, how they murmured up to the foot of palm trees under infinitely tall skies.

She remembered David saying wryly: "My people were Northerners as far back as we can trace it— Picts, Norse, Scots, sailors and crofters on the Atlantic edge—that must be why so many of them have become spacemen in the last several generations. To get away!"

And then, touching her hair with his lips: "But I've found what they were really looking for."

It was hard to imagine that David's warmth and tenderness and laughter had arisen in this tomb of a country. She had always thought of the religion which troubled him (he first came to know her through her father; professor and student had sat up many nights under Australian stars while David groped for a God not all iron and hellfire) as an alien stamp, as if the legendary Other Race Out There had once branded him. The obscurity of the sect had aided her: Christians were not uncommon, but she had vaguely imagined a Protestant was some kind of Moslem.

Now she saw that Skula's dwellers and Skula's God had come from Skula itself, with winter seas in their veins. David had not been struggling toward normality; he had been reshaping himself into something which—down underneath—Magnus Ryerson thought was not human. Suddenly, almost blindingly, Tamara remembered a few weeks ago, one night when the old man had set her a ballad to translate. "Our folk have sung it for many hundreds of years," he said—and how he had looked at her under his heavy brows.

> *"He hath taken off cross and iron helm,*
> *He hath bound his good horse to a limb,*
> *He hath not spoken Jesu name*
> *Since the Faerie Queen did first kiss him."*

Tamara struck a fist into one palm. The wind caught her cloak and peeled it from her, so that it flapped at her shoulders like black wings. She pulled it back around her, shuddering.

The sun was a red sliver on the world's rim. Darkness would come in minutes, thick enough for you to freeze to death fumbling your way home. Tamara began to walk, quickly, hoping to find a decision. She had not come out today just because the house was unendurable. But her mind had been stiff, as if rusted. She still didn't know what to do.

Or rather, she thought, *I do know, but haven't saved up the courage.*

When she reached the house, the air was already so murky she could almost not make out whitewashed walls and steep snow-streaked roof. A few yellow gleams of light came through cracks in the shutters. She paused at the door. To go in—! But there was no choice. She twisted the knob and stepped through. The wind and the sea-growl came with her.

"Close the door," said Magnus, "you little fool."

She shut out all but a mumble and whine under the eaves, hung her cloak on a peg and faced around. Magnus Ryerson sat in his worn leather chair with a worn leather-bound book in his hands. As always, as always! How could you tell one day from the next in this den? The radiglobe was turned low, making him mostly shadow, an icicle gleam of eyes and a dirty-white cataract of beard. A peat fire sputtered forlornly, trying to warm a teakettle on the hob.

Ryerson put the book down on his lap, knocked out his archaic pipe (it had turned the air foul in here) and asked roughly: "Where have you been all day, girl? I was about to go look for you. You could turn an ankle and die of exposure, alone on the ling."

"I didn't," said Tamara. She exchanged her boots for zori and moved toward the kitchen.

"Wait!" said Magnus. "Will you never learn? I want my high tea at just 1630 hours. . . . Now. You must be more careful, lass. You're carrying the last of the Ryersons."

Tamara stopped. On the downward slant of the ancient brick floor, she felt vaguely how her body braced itself. More nearly she felt how her chilled skin, which had begun to tingle as it warmed, grew numb again.

"Besides David," she said.

"If he is alive. Do you still believe it, after these weeks?" Magnus began scraping out his pipe. He did not look at her.

"I don't believe he is dead," she answered.

"The Lunar crew couldn't establish tach-beam contact. Supposing he is still alive, he'll die of old age before that ship reaches any star where men have an outpost. No, say rather he'll starve!"

"If he could repair whatever went wrong—"

The muffled surf-drums outside rolled up to a crescendo. Magnus tightened his mouth. "That is one way to destroy yourself . . . hoping," he said. "You must accept the worst, because there is always more of the worst than the best in this universe."

She glanced at the black book he called a Bible, heavy on one of the crowded shelves. "Do your holy writings claim that?'' she asked. Her voice came out as a stranger's croak.

"Aye. Likewise the second law of thermo-dynamics." Magnus knocked his pipe against the ashtray. It was an unexpectedly loud noise above the wind.

"And you . . . and you . . . won't even let me put up his picture," she whispered.

"It's in the album, with my other dead sons. I'll not have it on the wall for you to blubber at. Our part is to take what God sends us and still hold ourselves up on both feet."

"Do you know—" Tamara stared at him with a slowly rising sense of horror. "Do you know, I cannot remember exactly what he looked like?"

She had had some obscure hope of provoking his rage. But the shaggy-sweatered broad shoulders merely lifted, a shrug. "Aye, that's common enough. You've the words, blond hair and blue eyes and so on, but they make not any real image. Well, you didn't know him so very long, after all."

You are telling me I am a foreigner, she thought. *An interloper who stole what didn't belong to me.*

"We've time to review a little English grammar before tea," said the old man. "You've been terrible with the irregular verbs."

He put his book on the table—she recognized the title, Kipling's poems, whoever Kipling had been—and pointed at a shelf. "Fetch the text and sit down."

Something flared in the girl. She doubled her fists. "No."

"What?" The leather face turned in search of her.

"I am not going to study any more English."

"No—" Magnus peered as if she were a specimen from another planet. "Don't you feel well?"

She bit off the words, one after another: "I have

better ways to spend my time than learning a dead language."

"Dead?" cried the man. She felt his rage lift in the air between them. "The language of fifty million—"

"Fifty million ignorant provincials, on exhausted lands between bombed-out cities," she said. "You can't step outside the British Isles or a few pockets on the North American coast and have it understood. You can't read a single modern author or scientist or . . . or anybody . . . in English. I say it's dead! A walking corpse!"

"Your own husband's language!" he bawled at her, half rising.

"Do you think he ever spoke it to anyone but you, once he'd . . . he'd escaped?" she flung back. "Did you believe . . . if David ever returns from that ship you made him go on . . . and we go to Rama—did you imagine we'd speak the language of a dying race? On a new world?"

She felt the tears as they whipped down her face, she gulped after breath amidst terror. The old man was too hairy, too huge. When he stood up, the single radiglobe and the wan firelight threw his shadow across her and choked a whole corner of the room with it. His head bristled against the ceiling.

"So now your husband's race is dying," he said like a gun. "Why did you marry him, if he was that effete?"

"*He* isn't!" she called out. The walls wobbled around her. "You are! Sitting here in your dreams of the past, when your people ruled Earth—a past we're well out of! David was going where . . . where the future is!"

"I see." Magnus Ryerson turned half away from her. He jammed both fists into his pockets, looked down at the floor and rumbled his words to someone else—not her.

"I know. You're like the others, brought up to hate the West because it was once your master. Your teacher. The white man owned this planet a few centuries ago. Our sins then will follow us for the next thousand years . . . till your people fail in their turn, and the ones you raised up take revenge for the help they got. Well, I'm not going to apologize for my ancestors. I'm proud of them. We were no more vicious than the rest of mankind, and we gave . . . even on the deathbed of our civilization, we gave you the stars."

His voice rose until it roared. "And we're not dead yet! Do you think this miserable Protectorate is a society? It isn't! It's not even a decent barbarism. It's a glorified garrison. It's what's worshiping the status quo and afraid to look futureward. I went to space because my people once went to sea. I gave my sons to space, and you'll give yours to space, because that's where the next civilization will be! And you'll learn the history and the language of our people—your people—by God, you'll learn what it *means* to be one of us!"

His words rang away into emptiness. For a while only the wind and a few tiny flames had voice. Down on the strand, the sea worried the island like a terrier with a rat.

Tamara said finally: "I already know what it means. It cost me David, but I know."

He faced her again, lowered his head and stared as if at an enemy.

"You murdered him," she said, not loudly. "You sent him to a dead sun to die. Because you—"

"You're overwrought," he broke in with tight-held anger. "I urged him to try just one space expedition. And this one was important. It could have meant a deal to science. He would have been proud afterward, whatever he did for a career, to say, 'I was on the *Cross.*' "

"And he should die for his pride?" she said. "It's as senseless a reason as the real one. But I'll tell you why you made him go . . . and if you deny you forced him, I'll say you lie! You couldn't stand the idea that a child of yours had broken away—was not going to be wrenched into your image—had penetrated this obscene farce of space exploration, covering distance for its own sake, as if there were some virtue in a large number of kilometers. David was going to live as nature meant him to live, on a living soil, with un-tanked air to breathe and with mountains to walk on instead of a spinning coffin . . . and his children would too . . . we would have been happy! And that was what you couldn't stand to have happen!"

Magnus grinned without humor. "Yon's a lot of meaningless noise for a symbolics professor's daughter to make," he said. "To begin at the end, what proof have you we were meant to be happy?"

"What proof have you we were meant to jump across light-years?" she cried. "It's another way of running from yourself—no more. It's not even a practical thing. If the ships just looked for planets to colonize, I could understand. But . . . the *Cross* her-self was aimed for three giants! She was diverted to a black clinker! And now David is dead . . . for what? Scientific curiosity? You're not a research scientist, neither was he, and you know it. Wealth? He wasn't being paid more than he could earn on Earth. Glory? Few enough people on Earth care about exploration; not many more on Rama; he, not at all. Adventure? You can have more adventure in an hour's walk through a forest than in a year on a spaceship. I say you murdered your son because you saw him becoming sane!"

"Now that will do," growled Magnus. He took a step toward her. "I've heard enough out of you. In my own house. And I never did hold with this new-fangled notion of letting a woman yap—"

"Stand back!" she yelled. "I'm not *your* wife!"

He halted. The lines in his face grew suddenly blurred. He raised his artificial hand as if against a blow.

"You're my son's wife," he said, quite gently. "You're a Ryerson too . . . now."

"Not if this is what it means." She had found the resolution she sought. She went to the wall and took her cloak off its peg. "You'll lend me your aircar for a hop to Stornoway, I trust. I will send it back on autopilot and get transport for myself from there."

"But where are you going?" His voice was like a hurt child's.

"I don't know," she snapped. "To some place with a bearable climate. David's salary is payable to me till he's declared dead, and then there will be a pension. When I've waited long enough to be sure he won't come back, I'm going to Rama."

"But, lass—propriety—"

"Propriety be damned. I'd rather have David's child, alive."

She slipped her boots back on, took a flashlight from the cupboard, and went out the door. As she opened it, the wind came straight in and hit Magnus across the face.

13

"In the land of Chinchanchou,
*   Where the winds blow tender*
From a sea like purple wine
Foaming to defend her,
Lives a princess beautiful
*   (May the gods amend her!)*
Little known for virtue, but
*   Of most female gender."*

AS HE CAME around the gyro housing and pulled himself forward to the observation deck, David Ryerson heard the guitar skitter through half a dozen chords and Maclaren's voice come bouncing in its wake. He sighed, pushed the lank yellow hair back out of his eyes, and braced himself.

Maclaren floated in the living section. It was almost an insult to see him somehow clean, in a white tunic, when each man was allowed a daily spongeful of water for such purposes. And half rations had only leaned the New Zealander down, put angles in his smooth brown countenance; he didn't have bones jutting up under a stretched skin like Ryerson, or a flushed complexion and recurring toothache like Nakamura. It wasn't fair!

"Oh, hullo, Dave." Maclaren continued tickling his strings, but quietly. "How does the web progress?"

"I'm done."

"Hm?"

"I just clinched the last bolt and spotwelded the last connection. There's not a thing left except to find that germanium, make the transistors, and adjust the units." Ryerson hooked an arm around a stanchion and drifted free, staring out of sunken eyes toward emptiness. "God help me," he murmured, "what am I going to do now?"

"Wait," said Maclaren. "We can't do much else." He regarded the younger man for a while. "Frankly, both Seiichi and I found excuses not to help you, did less out there than we might have, for precisely that reason. I've been afraid you would finish the job before we found our planet."

Ryerson started. Redness crept into his chalky face. "Why, of all the—" His anger collapsed. "I see. All right."

"These weeks since we escaped have been an unparalleled chance to practice my music," remarked Maclaren. "I've even been composing. Listen."

> *"In their golden-masted ships*
> *Princes come a-wooing*
> *Over darkling spindrift roads*
> *Where the gales are brewing.*
> *Lusty tales have drawn them thence,*
> *Much to their undoing:*

When they seek the lady's hand
She gives them the ——"

"Will you stop that?" screamed Ryerson.

"As you like," said Maclaren mildly. He put the guitar back into its case. "I'd be glad to teach you," he offered.

"No."

"Care for a game of chess?"

"No."

"I wish to all the hells I'd been more of an intellectual," said Maclaren. "I never was, you know. I was a playboy, also in science. Now . . . I wish I'd brought a few hundred books with me. When I get back, I'm going to read them." His smile faded. "I think I might begin to understand them."

"When *we* get back?" Ryerson's thin frame doubled in mid-air as if for a leap. "*If* we get back, you mean!"

Nakamura entered. He had a sheaf of scribbled papers in one hand. His face was carefully blank. "I have completed the calculations on our latest data," he said.

Ryerson shuddered. "What have you found?" he cried. "For God's sake, what have you found?"

"Negative."

"Lord God of Israel," groaned Ryerson. "Negative again."

"That pretty well covers this orbit, then," said Maclaren calmly. "I've got the elements of the next one computed—somewhere." He went out among the instruments.

A muscle in Ryerson's cheek began to jump of itself. He looked at Nakamura for a long time. "Isn't there anything else we can do?" he asked. "The telescopes, the— Do we just have to *sit*?"

"We are circling a dead sun," the pilot reminded him. "We only have starlight to see by. A very powerful instrument might photograph a planet, but not our telescopes. Not at any distance greater than we could find them gravitationally. S-s-so.''

"We could make a big telescope!" exclaimed Ryerson. "We have glass, and . . . and silver and—"

"I've thought of that." Maclaren's tones drifted back from the observation section. "You're welcome to amuse yourself with it, but we'd starve long before a suitable mirror could be ground with the equipment here."

"But—Maclaren, space is so big! We could hunt for a million years and never find a planet if we can't . . . can't see them!"

"We're not working quite at random." Maclaren reappeared with a magnetic tape. "Perhaps you've forgotten the principle on which we are searching. We establish ourselves in an orbit about the star, follow it for a while, check our position repeatedly, and compute whether the path has been significantly perturbed. If it has been, that's due to a planet somewhere, and we can do a Leverrier to find that planet. If not—if we're too far away—we quarter to another arc of the same path and try again. Having exhausted a whole circumference thus, we move outward and try a bigger circle."

"Shut up!" rasped Ryerson. "I know it! I'm not a schoolboy, damn you! But we're *guessing*!"

"Not quite," said Maclaren. "You were occupied with the web when I worked out the secondary principle . . . yes, come to think of it, you never did ask me before. Let me explain. You see, by extrapolating from data on known stellar types, I know approximately what this star was like in its palmy days. From that, planetary-formation theory gives me the scale of its one-time system. For instance, its planets must have been more or less in the equatorial plane; such quantities as mass, angular momentum, and magnetic field determine the Bode's Law constants; to the extent that all this is known, I can draw an orbital map.

"Well, then the star went supernova. Its closer planets were whiffed into gas. The outermost giants would have survived, though badly damaged. But the semimajor axes of their orbits were so tremendous—theoretically, planets could have formed as much as a light-year from this star—that any small percentage of error in the data makes my result uncertain by Astronomical Units. Another factor: the explosion filled this space with gas. We're actually inside a nonluminous nebula. That would shorten the orbits of the remaining planets; in the course of millions of years they've spiraled far inward. In one way that helps us: we've an area to search which is not hopelessly huge. But on the other hand, just how long has it been since the accident? What's the density distribution of the nebula now, and what was it back then? I've taken some readings and made some estimates. All very crude, but—" Maclaren shrugged— "what else can we do? The successive orbits we have been trying are, more or less, those I have calculated for the surviving planets as of today. And, of course, intermediate radii to make sure that we will be measurably perturbed no matter where those planets actually are. It's a matter of getting close enough to one of them."

"If our food lasts," groaned Ryerson. "And we have to eat while we finish the web, too. Don't forget that."

"We're going to have to reorganize our schedules," said Maclaren thoughtfully. "Hitherto we've found things to keep us occupied. Now we must wait, and not go crazy waiting." He grinned. "I hereby declare the *Southern Cross* dirty-limerick contest open and offer a prize of—"

"Yes," said Ryerson. "Great sport. Fun and games, with Chang Sverdlov's frozen corpse listening in!"

Silence clapped down. They heard the air mumble in the ventilators.

"What else can we do with our poor friend?" asked Nakamura softly. "Send him on a test rocket into the black sun? He deserved better of us. Yes-s-s? Let his own people bury him."

"Bury a copy of him!" shrieked Ryerson. "Of all the senseless—"

"Please," said Nakamura. He tried to smile. "After all . . . it is no trouble to us, and it will comfort his friends at home, maybe yes? After all, speaking in terms of atoms, we do not wish to send ourselves back either. Only copies." He laughed.

"*Will you stop that giggling!*"

"Please." Nakamura pushed himself away, lifting astonished hands. "Please, if I have offended you, I am so sorry."

"So sorry! So sorry! Get out of here! Get out, both of you! I've seen more of you than I can stand!"

Nakamura started to leave, still bobbing his head, smiling and hissing in the shaftway. Maclaren launched himself between the other two. He snapped a hand onto either wrist.

"That will do!" They grew suddenly aware, it was shocking, how the eyes turned green in his dark hooked face. His words fell like axes. "Dave, you're a baby, screaming for mother to come change you. Seiichi, you think it's enough to make polite noises at the rest of the world. If you ever want to see sunlight again, you'll both have to mend your ideas." He shook them a little. "Dave, you'll keep yourself clean. Seiichi, you'll dress for dinner and talk with us. Both of you will stop feeling sorry for yourselves and start working to survive. And the next step is to become civilized again. We haven't got the size or the time or the force to beat that star: nothing but manhood. Now go off and start practicing how to be men!''

They said nothing, merely stared at him for a few moments and then departed in opposite directions. Maclaren found himself gazing stupidly at his guitar case. *I'd better put that away till it's requested,* he thought. *If ever. I didn't stop to think, my own habits might possibly be hard to live with.*

After a long time: *Seems I'm the new captain, in fact if not in name. But how did it happen? What have I done, what have I got?* Presently, with an inward twisting: *It must be I've less to lose. I can be more objective because I've no wife, no children, no cause, no God. It's easy for a hollow man to remain calm.*

He covered his eyes, as if to deny he floated among a million unpitying stars. But he couldn't hunch up that way for long. Someone might come back, and the captain mustn't be seen afraid.

Not afraid of death. Of life.

14

FROM A VIEW turret on the observation deck, the planet looked eerily like its parent star which had murdered it. Ryerson crouched in darkness, staring out to darkness. Against strewn constellations lay a gigantic black outline with wan streaks and edgings of gray. As he watched, Ryerson saw it march across the Milky Way and out of his sight. But it was the *Cross* which moved, he thought, circling her hope in fear.

I stand on Mount Nebo, he thought, *and down there is my Promised Land.*

Irrationally—but the months had made the crew odd, silent introverts, Trappists because meaningful conversation was too rare and precious to spill without due heed—he reached into his breast pocket. He took forth Tamara's picture and held it close to him. Sometimes he woke up breathing the fragrance of her hair. *Have a look,* he told her. *We found it.* In a heathen adoration: *You are my luck, Tamara. You found it.*

As the black planet came back into sight, monstrously swallowing suns (it was a bare thousand kilometers away), Ryerson turned his wife's image outward so she could see what they had gained.

"Are you there, Dave?"

Maclaren's voice came from around the cylinder of the living section. It had grown much lower in this time of search. Often you could scarcely hear Maclaren when he spoke. And the New Zealander, once in the best condition of them all, had lately gotten thinner than the other two, until his eyes stared from caves. But then, thought Ryerson, each man aboard had had to come to terms with himself, one way or another, and there had been a price. In his own case, he had paid with youth.

"Coming." Ryerson pulled himself around the deck, between the instruments. Maclaren was at his little desk, with a clipboard full of scrawled paper in one hand. Nakamura had just joined him. The Saraian had gone wholly behind a mask, more and more a polite unobtrusive robot. Ryerson wondered whether serenity now lay within the man, or the loneliest circle of hell, or both.

"I've got the data pretty well processed," said Maclaren.

Ryerson and Nakamura waited. The ship had seen curiously little exultation when the planet finally revealed itself. *I,* thought Ryerson, *have become a plodder. Nothing is quite real out here—there is only a succession of motions, in my body and my brain—but I can celebrate no victory, because there is none, until the final and sole victory: Tamara.*

But I wonder why Terangi and Seiichi didn't cheer?

Maclaren ruffled through his papers. "It has a smaller mass and radius than Earth," he said, "but a considerably higher density suggesting it's mostly nickel-iron. No satellite, of course. And, though the surface gravity is a bit more than Earth's, no atmosphere. Seems to be bare rock . . . or metal, I imagine. Solid, anyhow."

"How large was it once?" murmured Nakamura.

Maclaren shrugged. "That would be pure guesswork," he said. "I don't know which planet of the original system this is. One or two of the survivors may have crashed on the sun by now, you see. My personal guess, though, is that it was the 61 Cygni C type—more massive than Jupiter, though of less bulk because of core degeneracy. It had an extremely big orbit. Even so, the supernova boiled away its hydrogen and probably some of the heavier elements too. But that took time, and the planet still had this much mass left when the star decayed into a white dwarf. Of course, with the pressure of the outer layers removed, the core reverted to normal density, which must have been a pretty spectacular catastrophe in itself. Since then, the residual stellar gases have been making the planet spiral slowly inward, for hundreds of megayears. And now—"

"Now we found it," said Ryerson. "With three weeks' food supply to spare."

"And the germanium still to get," said Maclaren.

Nakamura drew a breath. His eyes went to the deck "beneath" his feet. Far aft was a storage compartment which had been left open to the bitterness of space; and a dead man, lashed to a stanchion.

"Had there been four of us," he said, "we would have consumed our supplies already and be starving. I am most humbly grateful to Engineer Sverdlov."

Maclaren's tone was dry. "He didn't die for that reason."

"No. But has he given us less, merely because it was an accident?"

They floated a while in stillness. Then Maclaren shook himself and said: "We're wasting time. This ship was never intended to land on a planet. Since I've already informed you any world we found might very likely use vacuum for sky, and you didn't object, I assume the aircraft can make a landing."

Nakamura crossed his legs and rested impassively, hands folded on his lap. "How familiar are you with the standard exploratory technique?" he inquired.

"Not very," confessed Maclaren. "I gather that aircraft are preferred for reasons of mass economy."

"And still more for maneuverability. A nuclear-powered vessel, using wings and turbojets, can rise high into an atmosphere, above the worst air resistance, without having to expend the reaction mass of a rocket. Likewise it can land more easily and safely in the first place. The aircraft which we carry, dismantled, are intended to leave their orbiting mother ship with a short jet burst, slip into the atmosphere of a new planet, and descend. The return is more difficult, of course, but they get into the stratosphere before applying the non-ionic rocket drive. This in turn takes them into space proper, where their ion accelerators will work. Naturally, the cabins being sealed, any kind of atmosphere will serve them.

"Now, this is for exploration purposes. But these auxiliary craft are also capable of landing on rockets alone. When the time has come to establish a beam-relay station, some airless, lifeless satellite is chosen, to avoid the necessity of quarantine. The craft shuttle back and forth, carrying the ship's dismantled transceiver. This is reassembled on the surface. Thereby the satellite's own mass becomes available to the matter bank, and any amount of material can be reconstructed according to the signals from the home station. The first things sent through are usually the parts for a much larger transceiver station, which can handle many tons of mass at a time.''

"Well, good," said Maclaren. "That was more or less what I thought. Let's land and—oh, oh."

Ryerson felt a smile tugging his lips, though it was not a happy one. "You see?" he murmured.

Maclaren regarded him closely. "You don't seem too discouraged," he said. "You must know an answer."

Ryerson nodded. "I've already spoken with Seiichi about it, while you were busy determining the exact characteristics of the planet. It's not going to be fun, but— Well, let him tell you."

Maclaren said slowly: "I had hoped, it was at least possible, that any planet we found would have a surviving satellite, small enough to land the whole ship on, or lay alongside if you want to consider it that way. It would have been the best thing for us. But I'm sure now that this lump has no companion of any kind. So we'll have to get our germanium down there."

"Which we could also have done, had we had the good luck to locate the planet sooner," Nakamura told him. "We can take aircraft down to the surface, yes. But we would have to transship all the mining and separating equipment, establish a working space and an airdome— It is too much work for three men to do before our three weeks of supplies are eaten up; and then the actual mining would remain."

Maclaren nodded. "I should have thought of this myself," he said. "I wonder how sane and sensible we are—how can we measure rationality, when we are all the human race we know for tens of light-years? —Well. I didn't think and you didn't talk. Nevertheless, I gather there's a way out of our dilemma."

"Yes," replied the pilot. "A riskful way, but any

other is certain death. We can take the ship down, and use her for our ready-made workshop and air-dome.''

''The *Cross*? But—well, of course the gravitation here is no problem to her, nor the magnetism now that the drive is shielded . . . but we can't make a tail landing, we'd crumple the web, and—hell's clanging bells, she can't land! She's not designed for it! Not maneuverable enough, why, it takes half an hour just to swing her clear around on gyros.''

Nakamura said calmly, ''I have made calculations for some time now, preparing for this eventuality. There was nothing we could do before knowing what we would actually find, but I do have some plans drawn up. We have six knocked-down auxiliary craft. Yes? It will not take long to assemble their non-ionic rocket drives, which are very simple devices, clamp these to the outside hull, and run their control systems through the ship's console. I think if we work hard we can have it assembled, tested, and functioning in two or three days. Each pair of rockets should be so mounted as to form a couple which will rotate the ship around one of the three orthogonal space axes. No? Thus the spaceship will become most highly responsive to piloting. Furthermore, we shall cut up the aircraft hulls, as well as whatever else we may need and can spare for this purpose, such as in-terior fittings. From this, we shall construct a tripod enclosing and protecting the stern assembly. It will be clumsy and unbalanced, of course—but I trust my poor maneuverings can compensate for that—and it will be comparatively weak—but with the help of radar and our powerful ion-blast, the ship can be landed quite gently.''

''Hm-m.'' Maclaren rubbed his chin. His eyes flickered between the other two faces. ''It shouldn't be hard to fix those rocket motors in place, as you say. But a tripod more than a hundred meters long, for a thing as massive as this ship—I don't know. If nothing else, how about the servos for it?''

"Please." Nakamura waved his words aside. "I realize we have not time to do this properly. My plan does not envision anything with self-adjusting legs. A simple, rigid structure must suffice. We can use the radar to select a nearly level landing place."

"All places are, down there," said Maclaren. "That iron was boiling once, and nothing has weathered it since. Of course, there are doubtless minor irregularities, which would topple us on our tripod—with a thousand tons of mass to hit the ground!"

Nakamura's eyes drooped. "It will be necessary for me to react quickly," he said. "That is the risk we take."

When the ship was prepared, they met once on the observation deck, to put on their spacesuits. The hull might be cracked in landing. Maclaren and Ryerson would be down at the engine controls, Nakamura in the pilot's turret, strapped into acceleration harness with only their hands left free.

Nakamura's gaze sought Maclaren's. "We may not meet again," he said.

"Possible," said Maclaren.

The small, compact body held steady, but Nakamura's face thawed. He had suddenly, after the long time which was gone, taken on an expression; and it was gentle.

"Since this may be my last chance," he said, "I would like to thank you."

"Whatever for?"

"I am not afraid any more."

"Don't thank me," said Maclaren, embarrassed. "Something like that, a chap does for himself, y' know."

"You earned me the time for it, at least."

Nakamura made a weightless bow. "*Sensei*, give me your blessing."

Maclaren said, with a degree of bewilderment: "Look here, everybody else has had more skill, contributed more, than I. I've told you a few things about the star and the planet, but you—Dave, at least—could have figured it out with slightly more difficulty. I'd never have known how to reconstruct a drive or a web, though; and I'd never be able to land this ship."

"I was not speaking of material survival," said Nakamura. A smile played over his mouth. "Still, do you remember how disorganized and noisy we were at first, and how we have grown so quiet since and work together so well? It is your doing. The highest interhuman art is to make it possible for others to use *their* arts." Then, seriously: "The next stage of achievement, though, lies within a man. You have taught me. Knowingly or not, Terangi-san, you have taught me. I would give much to be sure you will . . . have the chance . . . to teach yourself."

Ryerson appeared from the lockers. "Here they are," he said. "Tin suits for everybody."

Maclaren donned his armor and went aft. *I wonder how much Seiichi knows. Does he know that I've stopped making a fuss about things, that I didn't exult when we found this planet, not from stoicism but merely because I have been afraid to hope?*

I wouldn't even know what to hope for. All this struggle, just to get back to Earth and resume having fun? No, that's too grotesque.

"We should have issued the day's chow before going down," said Ryerson. "Might not be in any shape to eat it at the other end."

"Who's got an appetite under present circumstances?" said Maclaren. "So postponing dinner is one way of stretching out the rations a few more hours."

"Seventeen days' worth, now."

"We can keep going, foodless, for a while longer."

"We'll have to," said Ryerson. He wet his lips. "We won't mine our metal, and gasify it, and separate out the fractional percent of germanium, and make those transistors, and tune the circuits, in any seventeen days."

Maclaren grimaced. "Starvation, or the canned willy we've been afflicted with. Frankly, I don't expect much difference."

Hastily, he grinned at Ryerson, so the boy would know it for a jest. Grumbling was not allowed any more; they didn't dare. And the positive side of conversation, the dreaming aloud of "when we get home," had long since worn thin. Dinner-table conversation had been a ritual they needed for a while, but in a sense they had outgrown it. Now a man was driven into his own soul. *And that's what Seiichi meant,* thought Maclaren. *Only, I haven't found anything in myself. Or, no. I have. But I don't know what. It's too dark to see.*

He strapped himself in and began checking instruments.

"Pilot to engine room. Read off!"

"Engine room to pilot. Plus voltage clear. Minus voltage clear. Mercury flow standard . . ."

The ship came to life.

And she moved down. Her blast slowed her in orbit, she spiraled, a featureless planet of black steel called her to itself. The path was cautious. There must be allowance for rotation; there must not be too quick a change of velocity, lest the ponderous sphere go wobbling out of control. Again and again the auxiliary motors blasted, spinning her, guiding her. The ion-drive was not loud, but the rockets roared on the hull like hammers.

And down. And down.

Only afterward, reconstructing confused memories, did Maclaren know what had happened; and he was never altogether sure. The *Cross* backed onto an iron plain. Her tripod touched, on one foot, on two. The surface was not level. She began to topple. Nakamura lifted her with a skill that blended main drive and auxiliaries into a single smooth surge—such skill as an utterly relaxed man could achieve, responding to the immense shifting forces as a part thereof. He rose a few hundred meters, changed position relative to the ground, and tried anew. The tripod struck on two points once more. The ship toppled again. The third leg went off a small bluff, no more than a congealed ripple in the iron. It hit ground hard enough to buckle.

Nakamura raised ship barely in time. For an instant he poised in the sky on a single leg of flame, keeping his balance with snorts of rocket thrust. The bottom of the *Cross*' stern assembly was not many meters above ground.

Suddenly he killed the ion drive. Even as the ship fell, he spun her clear around on the rotator jets. The *Cross* struck nose first. The pilot's turret smashed, the bow caved in, automatic bulkheads slammed shut to save the air that whistled out. That was a great mass, and it struck hard. The sphere was crushed flat for meters aft of the bow. With her drive and her unharmed transceiver web aimed at the sky, the ship rested like Columbus' egg.

And the stars glittered down upon her.

Later Maclaren wondered: Nakamura might well have decided days beforehand that he would probably never be able to land any other way. Or he might have considered that his rations would last two men an extra week. Or perhaps, simply, he found his dark bride.

15

THE PLANET SPUN quickly about its axis, in less than ten hours. There went never a day across its iron plains, but hunger and the stars counted time. There was no wind, no rain, no sea, but a man's radio hissed with the thin dry talk of the stars.

When he stood at the pit's edge and looked upward, Maclaren saw the sky sharp and black and of an absolute cold. It had a somehow three-dimensional effect; theory said those crowding suns, blue-white or frosty gold or pale heatless red, were alike at optical infinity, but the mind sensed remoteness beyond remoteness, and whimpered. Nor was the ground underfoot a comfort, for it was almost as dark, starlit vision reached a few meters and was gulped down. A chopped-off Milky Way and a rising constellation (the one Maclaren had privately named Risus, the Sneer) told him that a horizon existed, but his animal instincts did not believe it.

He sighed, slapped a glare filter across his faceplate, and began cutting. The atomic hydrogen torch was lurid to look upon, but it jostled the stars out of his eyes. He cut rapidly, ten-kilo slabs which he kicked down into the pit so they wouldn't fuse tight again. The hole itself had originally been blasted, but the *Cross* didn't carry enough explosive for him to mine all his ore that way.

Ore, he reflected, was a joke. How would two men on foot prospect a sterilized world sealed into vacuum a hundred billion years ago? And there would have been little point in it. This planet had boiled once, at least on the surface; the metallic core itself had been heated and churned, quite probably to melting, when crushed atoms expanded to normal dimensions. The entire globe must be nearly uniform, one alloy lump. You took any piece, crushed it, gasified it, ionized it, put it through the electromagnetic isotope separator, and drew forth as much (or, rather, as minutely little) germanium as any other piece would have given you. From the known rate of extraction by such methods you could calculate when you would have four kilograms. The date lay weeks away.

Maclaren finished cutting, shut off his torch and hung it on its generator, and climbed into the bucket of the crane at the pit's edge. His flashbeam threw puddles of light on its walls as he was lowered. At the bottom he moved painfully about, loaded the bucket, and rode back to the surface. A small electric truck waited. He spilled the bucket into its box. And then it was to do again, and still again, until he had a full load.

Thank God and her dead designers, the *Cross* was well equipped for work on airless surfaces, she carried machines to dig and build and transport. But, of course, she had to. It was her main purpose, to establish a new transceiver station on a new moon; everything else could then come straight from the Solar System.

It had been her purpose.

Before heaven, it was yet.

Maclaren climbed wearily onto the truck seat. He and his spacesuit had a fourth again their Earth-weight here. His headlights picked out a line of paint leading toward the ship. It had been necessary to blast the pit some distance away, for fear of what ground vibrations might do to the web or the isotope separator. But then a trail had to be blazed, for nature had given no landmarks for guide; this ground was as bare as a skull.

Existence was like lead in Maclaren's bones.

After a while he made out the *Cross*, a flattened sphere crowned with a skeleton and the Orion nebula. It was no fun having everything upside down within her; a whole day had gone merely to reinstall the essential items. Well, Seiichi, you did what seemed best, and your broken body lies honored with Chang Sverdlov's, on the wide plains of iron.

Floodlights glared under the ship. Ryerson was finishing the previous load, reducing stone to pebbles and thence to dust. Good timing. Maclaren halted his truck and climbed down. Ryerson turned toward him. The undiffused glow reached through his faceplate and picked a sunken, bearded face out of night, little more than nose and cheekbone and bristling jaw. In his unhuman armor, beneath that cavernous sky, he might have been a troll. *Or I might,* thought Maclaren. *Humanity is far from us. We have stopped bathing, shaving, dressing, cooking . . . pretending; we work till our brains go blank, and then work some more, and crawl up the ladder into the ship for a few hours' uneasy sleep, and are*

*awakened by the clock, and fool our shriveled bellies
with a liter of tea, and put a lump of food in our
mouths and go out. For our time has grown thin.*

"Hello, Nibelung," said Ryerson.

Maclaren started. "Are you getting to be a
telepath?"

"It's possible," said Ryerson. His voice had
become a harsh whisper. His glance searched
darkness. "Anything is possible here."

"After we put this load through," said Maclaren,
evading the other thought, "we'd better move the
slag out of the ship. That ninety-nine-plus percent of
material we don't use piles up fast."

"M-hm." Ryerson clumped heavily to the truck
and began unloading. "And then out once more, cutting and loading and grinding and—merciful God,
but I'm tired! Do you really imagine we can keep on
doing heavy manual work like this, after the last food
has been eaten?"

"We'll have to," said Maclaren. "And, of course,
there is always—" He picked up a rock. Dizziness
whirled through him. He dropped the stone and sank
to his knees on the ground.

"Terangi!" Ryerson's voice seemed to come from
some Delphic deep, through mists. "Terangi, what's
wrong?"

"Nothing," mumbled Maclaren. He pushed at his
companion's groping arms. "Lea' me be . . . all right
in a minute. . . ." He relaxed against the stiffness of
armor and let his weakness go through him in tides.

After a while some strength returned. He looked
up. Ryerson was feeding the last rocks into the
crusher. The machine ate them with a growl that
Maclaren felt through the planet and his body. It
vibrated his teeth together.

"I'm sorry, Dave," he said.

"No harm. You should go up and bunk for a
while."

"Just a spell. Maybe we shouldn't have cut our rations as short as we have."

"You do seem to've been losing weight even faster than me," said Ryerson. "Maybe you ought to have an extra ration."

"Nah. It's metabolic inefficiency, brought on by well-spent years of wine, women, and off-key song."

Ryerson sat down beside him. "I'm a bit short of breath myself. Let's both take a break while the stuff goes through the crusher."

"Well," said Maclaren, "if your tailbone insulators can stand it, I suppose mine can."

They remained in silence for a while. The machine rumbled in their flesh and the stars muttered in their heads.

"How long do you think it will take to prepare the web?" asked Maclaren. "I mean, what's your latest estimate?"

"Hitherto I've underestimated the time for everything," said Ryerson. "Now, I simply don't know. First we'll have to get our germanium. Then, to make the units . . . I don't know. Two weeks, three? And then, once the circuits are functioning, they'll have to be tuned. Mostly by guesswork, since I don't really know the critical constants. That will take x time, depending on how lucky we are."

"We'll open the last packet of food soon," said Maclaren. In itself it was a totally useless reminder, but it was leading up to something they had both avoided.

Ryerson continued to squirm: "They say tobacco helps kill appetite."

"It does," said Maclaren, "but I smoked the last butts months ago. I've actually lost the addiction. Though of course I'll happily rebuild same the moment we strike Earth."

"When we come home . . ." Ryerson's voice drifted off like a murmur in sleep. "We haven't talked about our plans for a long time."

"It got to be too predictable, what every man would say."

"Yes. But is it now? I mean, do you still want to take that sailboat cruise around Earth, with . . . er . . . a female crew and a cargo of champagne?"

"I don't know," said Maclaren, faintly surprised to realize it. "I hadn't thought. . . . Do you remember once in space, we talked about our respective sailing experiences, and you told me the sea is the most inhuman thing on our planet?"

"Mm-m-m—yes. Of course, my sea was the North Atlantic. You might have had different impressions."

"I did. Still, Dave, it has stuck in my mind, and I see now you are right. Any ocean is, is too—big, old, blind for us—too beautiful." He sought the billion suns of the Milky Way. "Even this black ocean we're wrecked in."

"That's odd," said Ryerson. "I thought it was your influence making me think more and more of the sea as a—not a friend, I suppose. But hope and life and, oh, I don't know. I only know I'd like to take that cruise with you."

"By all means," said Maclaren. "I didn't mean I'd become afraid of the water, merely that I've looked a little deeper into it. Maybe into everything. Hard to tell, but I've had a feeling now and then, out here, of what Seiichi used to call insight."

"One does learn something in space," agreed Ryerson. "I began to, myself, once I'd decided that God hadn't cast me out here and God wasn't going to bring me back, it wasn't His part— Oh, about that cruise. I'd want to take my wife, but she'd understand about your, uh, companions."

"Surely," said Maclaren. "I'd expect that. You've told me so much about her, I feel like a family friend." *I feel as if I loved her.*

"Come around and be avuncular when we've set-
tled—Damn, I forgot the quarantine. Well, come see
our home on Rama in thirty years!"

Maclaren: *No, no, I am being foolish. The sky has
crushed me back toward child. Because she has
gallant eyes and hair like a dark flower, it does not
mean she is the one possible woman to fulfill that
need I have tried for most of my life to drown out. It
is only that she is the first woman since my mother's
death whom I realize is a human being.*

*And for that, Tamara, I have been slipping three-
fourths of my ration back into the common share, so
your man may innocently take half of that for his. It
is little enough I can do, to repay what you who I
never saw gave to me.*

"Terangi! You're all right, aren't you?"

"Oh. Oh, yes, of course." Maclaren blinked at the
other armored shape, shadowy beside him. "Sorry,
old chap. My mind wandered off on some or other
daisy-plucking expedition."

"It's an odd thing," said Ryerson. "I find myself
thinking more and more frivolously. Like this cruise
of yours, for instance. I really mean to join you, if
you stay willing, and we'll take that champagne
along and stop at every sunny island and loaf about
and have a hell of a good time. I wouldn't have expected this . . . what has happened . . . to change me
in that direction. Would you?"

"Why, no," said Maclaren. "Uh, I thought in fact
you—"

"I know. Because God seemed to be scourging me,
I believed the whole creation must lie under His
wrath. And yet, well, I have been on the other side of
Doomsday. Here, in nightmare land. And somehow,
oh, I don't know, but the same God who kindled that
nova saw equally fit to . . . to make wine for the wedding at Cana."

Maclaren wondered if the boy would regret so much self-revelation later. Perhaps not if it had been mutual. Hence he answered with care, "Oddly enough, or maybe not so oddly, my thinking has drifted in the opposite direction. I could never see any real reason to stay alive, except that it was more fun than being dead. Now I couldn't begin to list all the reasons. To raise kids into the world, and learn something about the universe, and not compromise with some crowned bastard's version of justice, and . . . I'm afraid I'm not a convert or anything. I still see the same blind cosmos governed by the same blind laws. But suddenly it matters. It matters terribly, and means something. What, I haven't figured out yet. I probably never will. But I have a reason for living, or for dying if need be. Maybe that's the whole purpose of life: purpose itself. I can't say. But I expect to enjoy the world a lot more."

Ryerson said in a thoughtful tone: "I believe we've learned to take life seriously. Both of us."

The grinder chuted its last dust into the receptacle. The gasifier was inboard; and the cold, not far from absolute zero, was penetrating the suit insulators. Ryerson got up. Shadows lapped his feet. "Of course," he said, his voice suddenly cracked, "that doesn't help us a great deal if we starve to death out here."

Maclaren rose with him. The floodlamps ridged both their faces against the huge hollow dark. Maclaren caught Ryerson's eyes with his own. For a moment they struggled, not moving under the constellations, and sweat sprang out upon Ryerson's forehead.

"You realize," said Maclaren, "that we actually can eat for quite a while longer. I'd say, at a guess, two more months."

"No," whispered Ryerson. "No, I won't."

"You will," Maclaren told him.

He stood there another minute, to make certain of his victory, which he meant as a gift to Tamara. Then he turned on his heel and walked over to the machine. "Come on," he said, "let's get to work."

16

MACLAREN WOKE UP of himself. At first he did not
remember where he was. He had been in some place
of trees, where water flashed bright beneath a hill.
Someone had been with him, but her name and face
would not come back. A warmth lingered on his lips.

He blinked at the table fastened to the ceiling. He
was lying on a mattress—

Yes. The *Southern Cross,* a chilly knowledge. But
why had he wakened early? Sleep was the last hiding
place left to him and Dave. They stood watch and
watch at the web controls, and came back to their
upside-down bunkroom and ate sleep. Life had
shrunken to that.

Maclaren yawned and rolled over. The alarm clock
caught his eye. Had the stupid thing stopped? He
looked at the second hand for a while, decided that it

was indeed moving. But then he had slept for—holy shark-toothed sea gods—for thirteen hours!

He sat up with a gasp. Bloodlessness went through his head. He clung to his blankets and waited for strength to come back. How long a time had it been, while his tissues consumed themselves for lack of all other nourishment? He had stopped counting hours. But the ribs and joints stuck out on him so he sometimes listened for a rattle when he walked. Had it been a month? At least it was a time spent inboard, with little physical exertion; that fact alone had kept him alive.

Slowly, like a sick creature, he climbed to his feet. If Dave hadn't called him, Dave might have passed out, or died, or proven to have been only a starving man's whim. *With a host of furious fancies—* Maclaren shambled across to the shaftway. The transceiver rooms were aft of the gyros; they had been meant to be "down" with respect to the observation deck during acceleration and now they were above him. Fortunately, the ship had been designed in the knowledge she would be in free fall most of her life. Maclaren gripped a rung with both hands. *I could use a little free fall,* he reflected through the dizziness. He put one foot on the next rung, used that leg and both hands to pull the next foot up beside it; now, repeat; once more; one for Father and one for Mother and one for Nurse and one for the cat and so it goes until here we are, shaking with exhaustion.

Ryerson sat at the control panel outside the receiving and transmitting chambers. It had been necessary to spotweld a chair, with attached ladder, to the wall and, of course, learn how to operate an upside-down control panel. The face that turned toward Maclaren was bleached and hairy and caved-in; but the voice seemed almost cheerful: "So you're awake."

"The alarm didn't call me," said Maclaren. He panted for air. "Why didn't you come rouse me?"

"Because I turned off the alarm in the first place."

"Huh?" Maclaren sat down on what had been the ceiling and stared upward.

"You'll fall apart if you don't get more rest," said Ryerson. "You've been in worse shape than me for weeks, even before the . . . the food gave out. I can sit here and twiddle knobs without having to break off every eight hours."

"Well, maybe." Maclaren felt too tired to argue.

"Any luck?" he asked after a while.

"Not yet. I'm trying a new sequence. Don't worry, we're bound to hit resonance soon."

Maclaren considered the problem for a while. Lately his mind seemed to have lost as much ability to hold things as his fingers. Painfully, he reconstructed the theory and practice of mattercasting. Everything followed with simple logic from the fact that it was possible at all.

Each tachyonic transceiver identified itself by a "carrier" pattern, of which the mattercasting signal was a set of modulations. The process only took place if contact had been established, that is, if the transmitter was emitting the carrier pattern of a functioning receiver. The 'caster itself, by the very act of scanning, generated the code which governed re-creation of the object transmitted. But first the 'caster must be tuned in on the desired receiving station.

The manual aboard ship gave the identifying pattern of every established transceiver: but, naturally, gave it in terms of the standardized and tested web originally built into the vessel. Thus, to reach Sol, the book said, blend your code with that for Rashid's Star, the nearest relay station in this particular case. Your signal will be automatically bucked on, through

several worlds, till it reaches Earth's Moon. Here are
the respective voltages, oscillator frequencies, etc.,
involved; have your computer total the resultant.

Ryerson's handmade web was not standardized.
He could put a known pattern into it, electronically,
but the tachyonics would then emit an unknown one,
the call signal of some station not to be built for the
next thousand years. He lacked instruments to
measure the relationship, so he could not recalculate
the appropriate settings. It was cut and try, with a
literal infinity of choices and just a few jackleg
estimates to rule out some of the possibilities.

Maclaren sighed. A long time had passed while he
sat thinking. Or so his watch claimed. He hadn't
noticed it go by, himself.

"You know something, Dave?" he said.

"Hm?" Ryerson turned a knob, slid a vernier one
notch, and punched along a row of buttons.

"We are out on the far edge of no place. I forget
how far to the nearest station, but a devil of a long
ways. This haywire rig of ours may not have the
power to reach it."

"I knew that all the time," said Ryerson. He
slapped the main switch. Needles wavered on dials,
oscilloscope tracings glowed elfhill green, it whined
in the air. "I think our apparatus is husky enough,
though. Remember, this ship has left Sol farther
behind than any other ever did. They knew she
would—a straight-line course would naturally outrun
the three-dimensional expansion of our territory—so
they built the transceiver with capacity to spare. Even
in its present battered state, it might reach Sol directly, if conditions were exactly right."

"Think we will? That would be fun."

Ryerson shrugged. "I doubt it, frankly. On a
statistical basis. There are too many other stations by
now— *Hey!*"

Maclaren found himself on his feet, shaking.

"What is it?" he got out. "What is it? For the love of heaven, Dave, what is it?"

Ryerson's mouth opened and closed, but no sounds emerged. He pointed with a bony arm. It shook.

Below him (it was meant to be above, like a star) a light glowed red.

"Contact," said Maclaren.

The word echoed through his skull as if spoken by a creator, across a universe still black and empty.

Ryerson began to weep, silently, his lips working. "Tamara," he said. "I'm coming home."

Maclaren thought: *If Chang and Seiichi had been by me now, what a high and proud moment.*

"Go on, Terangi," chattered Ryerson. His hands shook so he could not touch the controls. "Go on through."

Maclaren did not really understand it. Not yet. It was too swift a breaking. But the wariness of a race which had evolved among snakes and war spoke for him:

"Wait, Dave. Wait a minute. Let's be certain. Put a signal through. A teletype, I mean; we've no voice microphone, have we? You can do it right at that keyboard."

"What for?" screamed Ryerson. "What for? If you won't go through, I will!"

"Only wait." Suddenly Maclaren was begging. All the craziness of months between stars that burned his eyes woke up; he felt in a dim way that man must live under conditions and walk in awe, but this is one of the prides in being a man. He raised powerless hands and cried—it was not much above a whisper— "There could be distortion, you know. Accidents do happen, once in a great while, and this web was made by hand, half of it from memory. . . . Send a message. Ask for a test transmission back to us. It won't take long and . . . My God, Dave, what kind of thing could you send home to Tamara if the signal was wrong?''

Ryerson's chin quivered in its beard, but he punched the typer keys with hard angry strokes. Maclaren sat back down, breathing quickly and shallowly. So it was to become real. So he would again walk beneath the tall summer clouds of Earth.

No, he thought. *I never will. Terangi Maclaren died in an orbit around the black sun, and on the steel planet where it is always winter. The I that am may go home, but never the I that was.*

Ryerson bent over to look into the screen which gave him an image of the receiving chamber.

Maclaren waited. A long while passed.

''Nothing,'' said Ryerson. ''They haven't sent a thing.''

Maclaren could still not talk.

''A colonial station, of course,'' said Ryerson. ''Probably one of the outpost jobs with two men for a staff . . . or, Lord, another spaceship. Yes, that's likeliest, we're in touch with an interstellar. A single man on watch and—''

''And a bell ought to call him, shouldn't it?'' asked Maclaren, very slowly.

''You know how they get on the long haul,'' said Ryerson. He smote his chair arm with a fist that was all knobs. ''The man is sleeping too hard to hear a thing. Or—''

''Wait,'' said Maclaren. ''We've waited plenty long already. We can afford a few more minutes, to make certain.''

Ryerson blazed at him, as if he were an enemy. ''Wait, by jumping hell! No!''

He set the control timer for transmission in five minutes and crept from his seat and down the ladder. Under the soiled tunic, he seemed all spidery arms and legs, and one yellow shock of hair.

Maclaren rose again and stumbled toward him. "No," he croaked. "Listen, I realize how you feel, but I realize it's space lunacy too, and I forbid you, I forbid—"

Ryerson smiled. "How do you propose to stop me?" he asked.

"I—but can't you wait, wait and see and—"

"Look here," said Ryerson, "let's assume there is a freak in the signal. A test transmission comes through. At best, the standard object is distorted . . . at worst, it won't be recreated at all, and we'll get an explosion. The second case will destroy us. In the first case, we haven't time to do much more work. I doubt if I could climb around on the web outside any more. I know damn well you couldn't, my friend! We've no choice but to go through. Now!"

"If it's a ship at the far end, and you cause an explosion," whispered Maclaren, "you've murdered one more man."

Drearily, and as if from far away, he recognized the hardness which congealed the other face. Hope had made David Ryerson young again. "It won't blow up," said the boy, and was wholly unable to imagine such a happening.

"Well . . . probably not . . . but you still have the chance of molecular distortion or—" Maclaren sighed. Almost experimentally, he pushed at Ryerson's chest. Nothing happened; he was so much more starved that he could not move the lank body before him.

"Very well," said Maclaren. "You win. I'll go through."

Ryerson shook his head. "No, you don't," he answered. "I changed my mind." With a lilt of laughter: "I stand behind my own work, Terangi!"

"No, wait! Let me—I mean—think of your wife, at least—please—"

"I'll see you there," cried Ryerson. The blue glance which he threw over his shoulder was warm. He opened the transmitter room door, went through, it clashed shut upon him. Maclaren wrestled weakly with the knob. No use, it had an automatic lock.

Which of us is the fool? I will never be certain, whatever may come of this. The odds favor him, of course . . . in human terms, reckoned from what we know . . . but could he not learn with me how big this universe is, and how full of darkness?

Maclaren stumbled back toward the ladder to the chair. He would gain wrath, but a few more minutes, by climbing up and turning off the controls. And in those minutes, the strangely, terrifyingly negligent operator at the other end might read the teletype message and send a test object. And then Ryerson would know. Both of them would know. Maclaren put his feet on the rungs. He had only two meters to climb. But his hands would not lift him. His legs began to shake. He was halfway to the panel when its main switch clicked down and the transmitting engine skirled.

He crept on up. *Now I know what it means to be old,* he thought.

His heart fluttered feebly and wildly as he got into the chair. For a while he could not see the vision screens, through the night that spumed in his head. Then his universe steadied a little. The transmitter room was quite empty. The red light still showed contact. So at least no destruction had been wrought in the receiving place. Except maybe on Dave; it didn't take much molecular warping to kill a man. *But I am being timid in my weakness. I should not be afraid to die. Least of all to die. Let me also go on through and be done.*

He reached for the timer. His watch caught his eye. Half an hour since Dave left? Aready? Had it taken half an hour for him to creep this far and think a few sentences? But surely Dave would have roused even the sleepiest operator. They should have sent a teletype to the *Cross:* "Come on, Terangi. Come home with me." What was wrong?

Maclaren stared at the blank walls enclosing him. Here he could not see the stars, but he knew how they crowded the outside sky, and he had begun to understand, really understand what an illusion that was and how hideously lonely each of those suns dwelt.

One thing more I have learned, in this last moment, he thought. *I know what it is to need mercy.*

Decision came. He set the timer for ten minutes—his progress to the transmitter room would be very slow—and started down the ladder.

A bell buzzed.

His heart sprang. He crawled back, dimly feeling tears on his own face now, and stared into the screen.

A being stood in the receiving chamber. It wore some kind of armor, so he could not make out the shape very well, but though it stood on two legs the shape was not a man's. Through a transparent bubble of a helmet, where the air within bore a yellowish tinge, Maclaren saw its face. Not fish or frog or mammal, it was so other a face that his mind would not wholly register it. Afterward he recalled only blurred features, tendrils and great red eyes.

Strangely, beyond reason, in that first look he read compassion on the face.

The creature bore David Ryerson's body in its arms.

17

WHERE SUNDA STRAITS lay beneath rain (but
sunlight came through to walk upon the water) the
land fell steep. It was altogether green; in a million
subtle hues, jungle and plantation and rice paddy, it
burned with leaves. White mists wreathed the peak of
a volcano, and was it thunder across wind or did the
mountain talk in sleep?

Terangi Maclaren set his aircar down on brown-
and-silver water and taxied toward the Sumatra
shore. Each day he regained flesh and strength, but
the effort of dodging praus and pontoon houses and
submarines still tired him. When his guide pointed:
"There, tuan," he cut the engines and glided in with
a sigh.

"Are you certain?" he asked, for there were many

such huts of thatch and salvaged plastic along this coast. It was a wet world here, crowding brown folk who spent half their cheerful existences in the water, divers, deckhands, contracting their labor to the sea ranches but always returning home, poverty, illiteracy, and somehow more life and hope than the Citadel bore.

"Yes, tuan. Everyone knows of her. She is not like the rest, and she holds herself apart. It marks her out."

Maclaren decided the Malay was probably right. Tamara Suwito Ryerson could not have vanished completely into the anonymous proletariat of Earth. If she planned to emigrate, she must at least leave a mailing address with the Authority. Maclaren had come to Indonesia quickly enough, but there his search widened, for a hundred people used the same P.O. in New Djakarta and their homes lay outside the cosmos of house numbers and phone directories. He had needed time and money to find this dwelling.

He drove up onto the shore. "Stay here," he ordered his guide, and stepped out. The quick tropic rain poured over his tunic and his skin. It was the first rain he had felt since . . . how long? It tasted of morning.

She came to the door and waited for him. He would have known her from the pictures, but not the grace with which she carried herself. She wore a plain sarong and blouse. The rain filled her crow's-wing hair with small drops and the light struck them and shattered.

"You are Technic Maclaren," she said. He could scarcely hear her voice, so low did it fall, but her eyes were steady on his. "Welcome."

"You have seen me on a newscast?" he inquired, banally, for lack of anything else.

"No. I have only heard. Old Prabang down in the

village has a nonvisual set. But who else could you
be? Please come in, sir.''

Later he realized how she broke propriety. But
then, she had declared herself free of Protectorate
ways months ago. He found that out when he first
tried to contact her at her father-in-law's. The hut,
within, was clean, austerely furnished, but a vase of
early mutation-roses stood by David's picture.

Maclaren went over to the cradle and looked down
at the sleeping infant. ''A son, isn't it?'' he asked.

''Yes. He has his father's name.''

Maclaren brushed the baby's cheek. He had never
felt anything more soft. ''Hello, Dave,'' he said.

Tamara squatted at a tiny brazier and blew up its
glow. Maclaren sat down on the floor.

''I would have come sooner,'' he said, ''but there
was too much else, and they kept me in the
hospital—''

''I understand. You are very kind.''

''I . . . have his effects . . . just a few things. And I
will arrange the funeral in any way you desire and—''
His voice trailed off. The rain laughed on the thatch.

She dipped water from a jar into a teakettle. ''I
gather, then,'' she said, ''you bring no letter that he
wrote?''

''No. Somehow . . . I don't know. For some
reason none of us wrote any such thing. Either we
would all perish out there, and no one else would
come for fifty or a hundred years, or we would get
back. We never thought it might be like this, a single
man.'' Maclaren sighed. ''It's no use trying to
foresee the future. It's too big.''

She didn't answer him with her voice.

''But almost the last thing Dave said,'' he finished
awkwardly, ''was your name. He went in there
thinking he would soon be home with you.''
Maclaren stared down at his knees. ''He must

have—have died quickly. Very quickly."

"I have not really understood what happened," she said, kneeling in the graceful Australian style to set out cups. Her tone was flattened by the effort of self-control. "I mean, the 'cast reports are always superficial and confused, and the printed journals too technical. There isn't any middle ground any more. That was one reason we were going to leave Earth, you know. Why I still am going to, when our baby has grown a little bit."

"I know how you feel," said Maclaren. "I feel that way myself."

She glanced up with a startled flirt of her head that was beautiful to see. "But you are a technic!" she exclaimed.

"I'm a human being too, my lady. But go on, ask me your question, whatever you were leading toward. I've a favor of my own to ask, but you first."

"No, what do you want? Please."

"Nothing important. I've no claim on you, except the fact that your husband was my friend. I'm thinking of what you might do for his sake. But it will wait. What did you wonder about?"

"Oh. Yes. I know you tuned in the aliens' transceiver and didn't realize it. But—" Her fists clenched together. She stared through the open door, into the rain and the light, and cried forth: "It was such a tiny chance! Such a meaningless accident that killed him!"

Maclaren paused until he had his words chosen. Then he said, as gently as might be:

"It wasn't so wildly improbable. All this time we've known that we couldn't be the only race reaching for the stars. It was absurd to think so; that would have been the senseless unlikelihood. Well, the *Cross* was farther out than men had ever gone before, and the alien spaceship was near the aliens' own limit of expansion. It was also bound for Alpha Crucis. Odd what a sense of kinship that gives me, my brother mariner, with chlorine in his lungs and silicon in his bones, steering by the same lodestar. Contact was certain eventually, as they and we came into range of each other's signals. Your David was the man who first closed the ring. We were trying call patterns we could not measure, running through combinations of variables. Statistically, we were as likely to strike one of their patterns as one of ours."

The water began to boil. She busied herself with the kettle. The long tresses falling past her face hid whether she was crying or not. Maclaren added for her, "Do you know, my lady, I think we must have called hundreds of different space-traveling races. We were out of their range, of course, but I'm sure we called them."

Her voice was muffled: "What did the aliens think of it?"

"I don't know. In ten years we may begin to talk to them. In a hundred years, perhaps we will understand them. And they us, I hope. Of course, the moment David . . . appeared . . . they realized what had happened. One of them came through to me. Can you imagine what courage that must have taken? How fine a people your man has given us to know? There was little they could do for me, except test the *Cross'* web and rule out the call patterns which they use. I kept on trying, after that. In a week I finally raised a human. I went through to his receiver and that's all. Our technicians are now building a new relay station on the black star planet. But they'll leave the *Cross* as she is, and David Ryerson's name will be on her."

"I thought," she whispered, still hiding her face, "that you . . . I mean, the quarantine rules—"

"Oh, yes, the Protectorate tried to invoke them.

Anything to delay what is going to happen. But it was useless. Nothing from the aliens' planet could possibly feed on Terrestrial life. That's been established already, by the joint scientific commission; we may not be able to get the idea behind each other's languages yet, but we can measure the same realities! And of course, the aliens know about us. Man just can't hide from the universe. So I was released." Maclaren accepted the cup she offered him and added wryly: "To be sure, I'm not exactly welcome at the Citadel any more."

She raised large eyes to him. He saw how they glimmered. "Why not?" she asked. "You must be a hero to—"

"To spacemen, scientists, some colonials, and a few Earthmen glad of an end to stagnation. Not that I deserve their gratitude. Three dead men really did this. But at any rate, my lady, you can foresee what an upheaval is coming. We are suddenly confronted with— Well, see here, the aliens must be spread through at least as large a volume of space as man. And the two races don't use the same kind of planets. By pooling transceiver networks, we've doubled both our territories! No government can impose its will on as many worlds as that.

"But more. They have sciences, technologies, philosophies, religions, arts, insights which we never imagined. It cannot be otherwise. And we can offer them ours. How long do you think this narrow little Protectorate and its narrow little minds can survive such an explosion of new thought?" Maclaren leaned forward. He felt it as an upsurge in himself. "My lady, if you want to live on a frontier world, and give your child a place where it's hard and dangerous and challenging—and everything will be possible for him, if he's big enough—stay on Earth. The next civilization will begin here on Earth herself."

Tamara set down her cup. She bent her face into

her hands and he saw, helpless, how she wept. "It may be," she said to him, "it may be, I don't know. But why did it have to be David who bought us free? Why did it have to be him? He didn't mean to. He wouldn't have, if he'd known. I'm not a sentimental fool, Maclaren-san, I know he only wanted to come back here. And he died! There's no meaning in it!"

18

THE NORTH ATLANTIC rolled in from the west, gray and green and full of thunder. A wind blew white manes up on the waves. Low to the south gleamed the last autumnal daylight, and clouds massed iron-colored in the north, brewing sleet.

"There," pointed Tamara. "That is the place."

Maclaren slanted his aircar earthward. The sky whistled around him. So Dave had come from here. The island was a grim enough rock, harshly ridged. But Dave had spoken of gorse in summer and heather in fall and lichen of many hues.

The girl caught Maclaren's arm. "I'm afraid, Terangi," she whispered. "I wish you hadn't made me come."

"It's all we can do for David," he told her. "The

last thing we'll ever be able to do for him.''

"No." In the twilight, he saw how her head lifted. "Things never end. Not really. His child and mine, waiting, and— At least *we* can put a little sense into life.''

"I don't know whether we do or whether we find what was always there," he replied. "Nor do I care greatly. To me, the important thing is that the purpose—order, beauty, spirit, whatever you want to call it—does exist.''

"Here on Earth, yes," she sighed. "A flower or a baby. But then three men die beyond the sun, and it so happens the race benefits a little from it, but I keep thinking about all those people who simply die out there. Or come back blind, crippled, broken like dry sticks, with no living soul the better for it. Why? I've asked it and asked it, and there isn't ever an answer, and finally I think that's because there isn't any why to it in the first place.''

Maclaren set the car down on the beach. He was still on the same search, along a different road. He had not come here simply to offer David's father whatever he could: reconciliation, at least, and a chance to see David's child now and then in the years left him. Maclaren had some obscure feeling that an enlightenment might be found on Skula.

Truly enough, he thought, men went to space, as they had gone to sea, and space destroyed them, and still their sons came back. The lure of gain was merely a partial answer; spacemen didn't get any richer than sailors had. Love of adventure . . . well, in part, in some men, and yet by and large the conquerors of distance had never been romantics, they were workaday folk who lived and died among sober realities. When you asked a man what took him out to the black star, he would say he had gone under orders, or that he was getting paid, or that he was curious about it, or any of a hundred reasons. Which might all be true. And yet was any of them the truth?

And why, Maclaren wondered, did man, the race, spend youth and blood and treasure and every high hope upon the sea and the stars? Was it only the outcome of meaningless forces—economics, social pressure, maladjustment, myth, whatever you labeled it—a set of chance-created vectors with the sardonic resultant that man broke himself trying to satisfy needs which could have been more easily and sanely filled at home?

If I could get a better answer than that, thought Maclaren, *I could give it to Tamara. And to myself. And then we could bury our dead.*

He helped her out of the car and they walked up a path toward the ancient-looking cottage. Light spilled from its windows into a dusk heavy with surf. But they had not quite reached it when the door opened and a man's big form was outlined.

"Is that you, Technic Maclaren?" he called.

"Yes. Captain Magnus Ryerson?" Maclaren stepped ahead of Tamara and bowed. "I took the liberty, sir, of bringing a guest with me whom I did not mention when I called."

"I can guess," said the tall man. "It's all right, lass. Come in and welcome."

As she passed over the uneven floor to a chair, Tamara brushed Maclaren and took the opportunity to whisper: "How old he's grown!"

Magnus Ryerson shut the door again. His hands, ropy with veins, shook a little. He leaned heavily on a cane as he crossed the room and poked up the fire. "Be seated," he said to Maclaren. "When I knew you were coming, I ordered some whisky from the mainland. I hope it's a good make. I drink not, you see, but be free to do so yourself."

Maclaren looked at the bottle. He didn't recognize

the brand. "Thank you," he said, "that's a special
favorite of mine."

"You've eaten?" asked the old man anxiously.

"Yes, thank you, sir." Maclaren accepted a glass.
Ryerson limped over the floor to give Tamara one.

"Can you stay the night? I've extra beds in the
garret, from when the fisher lads would come by.
They come no more, no reason for it now, but I've
kept the beds."

Maclaren traded a look with Tamara. "We would
be honored," he said.

Magnus Ryerson shuffled to the hob, took the
teakettle, poured himself a cup and raised it. "Your
health." He sat down in a worn chair by the fire. His
hands touched a leather-bound book lying on its
arm.

There was silence for a while, except that they
could hear the waves boom down on the strand.

Maclaren said finally: "I . . . we, I mean . . . we
came to—to offer our sympathy. And if I could tell
you anything . . . I was there, you know."

"Aye. You're kind." Ryerson groped after a pipe.
"It is my understanding he conducted himself well."

"Yes. Of course he did."

"Then that's what matters. I'll think of a few
questions later, if you give me time. But that was the
only important one."

Maclaren looked around the room. Through its
shadows he saw pilot's manuals on the shelves,
stones and skins and gods brought from beyond the
sky; he saw the Sirian binary like twin hells upon
darkness, but they were very beautiful. He offered:
"Your son was in your own tradition."

"Better, I hope," said the old man. "There would
be little sense to existence, did boys have no chance to
be more than their fathers."

Tamara stood up. "But that's what there isn't!"

she cried. "There's no sense! There's just dying and dying and dying—what for?—so we can walk on still another planet, learn still another fact—what have we gained? What have we really done? And why? In your own God's name, what did we do once that He sends our men out there now?"

She clamped her hands together. They heard how the breath rasped in her. She said at last, "I'm sorry," and sat back down. Her fingers twisted blind until Maclaren took them.

Magnus Ryerson looked up. And his eyes were not old. He let the surf snarl on the rocks of his home for a while. And then he answered her: *" 'For that is our doom and our pride.' "*

"What?" She started. "Oh. In English. Terangi, he means—" She said it in Interhuman.

Maclaren sat quite still.

Ryerson opened his book. "They have forgotten Kipling now," he said. "One day they will remember. For no people live long, who offer their young men naught but fatness and security. Tamara, lass, let your son hear this one day. It is his song too, he is human."

The words were unknown to Maclaren, but he listened and thought that in some dark way he understood.

> *" 'We have fed our sea for a thousand years*
> *   And she calls us, still unfed,*
> * Though there's never a wave of all her waves*
> *   But marks our English dead:*
> * We have strawed our best to the weed's unrest,*
> *   To the shark and the sheering gull.*
> * If blood be the price of admiralty,*
> *   Lord God, we ha' paid in full!' "*

When Ryerson had finished, Maclaren stood up, folded his hands and bowed. *"Sensei,"* he said, "give me your blessing."

"What?" The other man leaned back into shadows, and now he was again entirely old. You could scarcely hear him under the waves outside. "You've naught to thank me for, lad."

"No, you gave me much," said Maclaren. "You have told me why men go, and it isn't for nothing. It is because they are men."